MW01230879

The Crystal Clipper

The Crystal Clipper

The Fairy Tale

Book One of The Moon Singer

B. Roman

Published 2016 by Creativia

Book design by Creativia (www.creativia.org)

Cover Design by http://www.thecovercollection.com/

Prologue

"And how shall I come to Earth this time, in what form and which incarnation? Do I have the will to try again?"

Other: Of course, *here* there is no "will" – there is only doing, being, and knowing.

"But I have so grown tired of the journeys, the repetitious teaching of the same lesson over and over again, only to be disappointed by resistance."

Other: Then teach a new lesson, or the same Truth, in a new way. Until it is imbued into bodies, minds and hearts, and then believed, you will continue to make the sojourns.

"A multitude of times, I have made my presence felt but not known, not revealing who or what I am. Isn't it time to do so? Reveal, that is?"

Other: It depends on your subject. Would he or she be ready to accept this knowledge?

"There could be danger there, if the knowledge is used unwisely, or with self-serving motives. My... *the* subject... best for receiving would be someone who has a grand purpose beyond his or her own fulfillment."

Other: An innocent, perhaps. Someone who has never thought to seek such knowledge - yet.

"But where will this One be found?"

Other: In the past and present, in the heavens and on earth, in time and space. And in his mother's heart.

"Mother's heart?"

Other: In recognizing *her* heart's desire, you will find this One that you seek, whose own purpose you will recognize immediately.

"And that is…?"

Other: To save a life that means more to him than his own.

"But how shall I reveal myself to him?"

Other: Uniquely. In a most extraordinary and magnificent way.

One

At the age of seven David Nickerson's lively, joyous world went silent. The surf roaring only steps from his front door, his mother's sweet voice, the cries and squeals of his little sister, the stern teachings of his father, his Aunt Dorothy's rip-roaring laughter - were sounds he could no longer hear. They were, nonetheless, indelibly imprinted in his heart and memory, never to be forgotten.

Little did David suspect that in the ensuing years his disability would become his greatest asset. Never in his wildest dreams did he imagine that his hearing aid would become an instrument for telepathic communication. And if anyone had told him that one day he would travel to worlds beyond this one, and experience the past, present and future as one, he would have said they were crazy.

The startling events that will change David's life forever are mere hours away, but the means of transport that will take him to worlds unexplored is not an ordinary vehicle. It fits in the palm of his hand, yet can travel to the endless reaches of time and space on a journey that only the soul can take. As guardian of this coveted prize, David will learn that he is not only blessed, but cursed; there are others who are willing to die for it and to kill for it. For whoever possesses *The Moon Singer* and learns its secrets will control the fate of the world.

But, what about David's fate? Which world will he choose to live in – the world of fantasy or reality? The "other world" of hearing or his "real-time" world of silence? And what will be the full consequences of his choice? In the end, will he really have a choice?

One always does...

Port Avalon, June

David Nickerson studies his newest treasure, holding it between his thumb and forefinger. The sunlight shining through the open parlor window reflects on each of the gem's perfect planes. Its mysterious beauty dazzles him.

"Holy Cow. I've never seen anything like it, Aunt Dorothy. What kind of crystal is it?" After years of practice, David speaks with barely an impediment. The special hearing aid he uses enables him to hear his own vocal vibrations but not discernable words. Still, it gives him a connection to the resonating world around him. The illness that took David's hearing was a grave one, but his spirit prevailed. He worked tirelessly to become a champion signer, an expert lip reader, determined not to let his deafness limit him. For, in all other ways, David was a normal boy - bright, curious, athletic, strong willed. Every summer, he spent hours in the sun surfing and swimming, tanning his skin bronze from head to toe, his blond hair bleached almost white.

In school, his penchant for music coincided nicely with his interest in science and computers. Yet, in somewhat of a paradox, David also grew to love the romance of metaphysics, especially the mystical and mythical powers of crystals.

"It's called a Singer," Dorothy says, and signs the word *Singer*.

"Why do they call it that?" David stares intently at his aunt to read every word on her lips. Dorothy is an adequate signer but struggles to communicate the intricacies of the gem's description, and so combines words and sign language.

"Each crystal in the cluster contains its own unique vibration," she tells him, "but joined together like this they create a symphony of sounds that literally sing the answers to all the mysteries in the universe. Or so the legend goes."

"I bet it's thousands, maybe millions of years old," David figures.

The crystal sparkles pure and translucent one minute, a rainbow mosaic the next. It is a jigsaw arrangement of atoms, a harmonic conversion of energy and matter. Yet, it looks amazingly like a primitive sculpture fashioned by someone in love with the sea.

"It's incredible. Look at it, Aunt Dorothy. Its microstructure is so complex. But what really amazes me is its shape. It looks like a miniature ship. Here's the mast where the sail would go, and here's the bow, the stern and the rudder."

Dorothy adds more impetus to the Singer's mystique. "If its owner believes in it, and works with its energy, he will develop extraordinary powers of communication, clairvoyance and prophecy."

"Hogwash," Isaac Nickerson scoffs without looking up from his evening newspaper. "It's a rock, like all the other so-called magic crystals you've given the boy. Stop filling his head with nonsense."

David cocks his head and looks at Dorothy questioningly. He was not able to read his father's lips, but he senses his displeasure. Dorothy signs, "Old Fogey." David stifles a chuckle.

"Just because you don't agree with something doesn't mean it's nonsense, Isaac," Dorothy needles her brother. "Besides, we all need a little myth and magic in our lives. It gives us hope."

"The only hope we have is hard work and accepting our lot in life. There are no amulets to protect us from harm, and no talismans to bring us good luck." Isaac folds his newspaper with an agitated snap and drops it in the basket beside his chair. He rises to leave the room, but Dorothy presses the debate further.

"Is that why you light that old oil lamp on the porch each night to welcome home sailors who no longer sail?"

"You know that lamp light has been a tradition in our family for 200 years. It's symbolic," Isaac defends his nightly ritual.

Dorothy winks at David. She's going to drive another one home. "One man's tradition is another man's superstition. And what about Father's gold watch fob? Why do you always wear it when you ask Fischbacher for a raise?"

"That fob is the only heirloom Father was able to leave me after years of giving his blood, sweat and tears to Fischbacher and this town. I am fond of it, but I certainly don't consider it a lucky piece, not in the least."

Isaac leaves the house abruptly and walks out to the pier that extends from the front of the Nickerson's historic Victorian home. He stands there, pensively gazing out at the sea. The afternoon breeze is impotent and barely stirs the small flag atop a buoy that bobs lazily on the water. The usually peaceful sounds - the squawking of sea gulls, the dinging bell of a slow-moving barge approaching the harbor - seem melancholy now. The despairing idleness of the town mirrors Isaac's mood on this summer day.

David expels a helpless sigh. "Dad's in no mood to spar with you today, Aunt Dorothy. Fischbacher refused to give him the loan for Sally's operation."

"What? Why, the old tightwad."

"My feelings exactly. Dad even offered to sign a paper agreeing to any terms Fischbacher wanted."

"Signing a contract drawn up by Nathan Fischbacher would be committing financial suicide. The man is an unethical *snake*." Dorothy hisses the word through tight teeth. "Still, if he knew he'd get paid back, why did he refuse your father the loan?"

David removes a document from the desk drawer and hands it to Dorothy. She reads it, then sinks into her brother's easy chair.

"Oh, no. I can't believe it. Selling the company after all these years."

"Yeah. Selling the company and letting everyone go at the end of the month. And without a job, Dad could never pay back the loan."

"Or get one anywhere else."

"Please don't say anything to Sally. Dad doesn't want her to know yet."

"Maybe the new owners will keep him on. He's the best draftsman in the business." Despite their sibling rivalry, Dorothy is proud of her younger brother's accomplishments. "Surely they can use him."

"If they're smart they will, but Dad doesn't think there's much chance of that. They're only buying Fischbacher's company to eliminate the competition, not to expand." "And Fischbacher will rake in more millions, as if he needs it, the greedy reptile.

What a waste, putting all those people out of work. They'll never find new jobs in this lifeless old town."

David searches through the oversized file cabinet next to his father's drafting table, then pulls out a set of blueprints and opens them up to full size. "Look at these, Aunt Dorothy."

"What are they?"

"Designs Dad has been working on for laser-powered cargo ships. They're sleek and clean, more fuel efficient, and more powerful than anything Fischbacher has now. These ships would revolutionize the business. They could cut expenses and increase profits dramatically in just a few months."

"Has Isaac shown these designs to Fischbacher?"

"Dad gave Fischbacher a whole set of them. He keeps promising he'll look them over, but he never does." David refolds the blueprints and replaces them in the files.

"Mom's dying was hard enough on him. And now with the worry over Sally's operation, Dad's just about given up on everything." He slams the drawer shut. "Damn! It's just not fair! Dad deserves to be recognized for his work. And Sally…" David's voice softens. "Sally deserves to get out of that wheelchair and walk again, to go to the prom in a pretty dress and dance all night, like…"

"Like a princess," Dorothy completes David's wish.

"Yeah. Like a princess. I feel so helpless, Aunt Dorothy. Maybe I should quit school and get a full-time job." The thought deflates him.

"You'll do no such thing, David Nickerson. You need that diploma to get into college. You don't want to wind up being a cook on a freighter like your old aunt."

"I could do worse," he says fondly. He loves his aunt. She is still vital and attractive at age 60, with a mind as agile and curious as David's. "I mean, you get to travel all over the world and bring me back wonderful treasures."

Dorothy takes David by the hand and leads him to the sofa where they sit, side by side. "It's not as glamorous as you think," Dorothy confesses, then laughs at herself. "Beats me why I still do it at my age. And I certainly haven't contributed much to the world. But you – you have the special gifts that can make things happen, that can change the world for the better. And a solid education is just the beginning for you."

"I'm not sure my physics teacher would agree with you after my dismal final exam."

"Well, maybe I've visited too many psychics and fortune tellers, but I just have a gut feeling that your insights transcend this little old Earth plane, but they have yet to be tapped. Most people are too afraid to explore the depths of their soul, and they wander aimlessly through life feeling helpless. Meanwhile, the unscrupulous seize all the power and use it to their own benefit."

"You mean like Nathan Fischbacher."

Dorothy nods. "Exactly."

"But his power is his meanness, not to mention his money. How could exploring my soul teach me to outsmart a creep like him? They don't teach that in physics class."

"Truth is knowledge, and knowledge is power, David." She signs the words *truth*, *power*, and *courage* as she speaks. "It not only takes great courage to seek the truth, it's also a responsibility not to be taken lightly."

Truth-seeking is a sojourn that David equates with King Arthur's quest for the Holy Grail. The thought overwhelms him. "I've got all I can do to handle the normal stuff, Aunt Dorothy. I'm no Sir Lancelot."

Dorothy hugs her nephew fiercely and kisses his cheek. "I've got to go now." She gathers up her purse and sunglasses, then moves to the table where all of David's crystals are laid out side by side. She picks up the Singer and presses it into his hand.

"Don't give up hope, David. If anyone can find magic in these beautiful crystals, you can. But remember, it must only be used for good."

Dorothy leaves the house and joins Isaac on the pier, slipping her arm affectionately through his. David's heart warms at this sight, and he can't help but smile despite his anguish.

Scanning the parlor, he seems to truly see its history for the first time. It is filled with functional antiques, sturdy furnishings handed down from generation to generation and still used proudly. Memorabilia and artifacts, collected by the Nickerson family during centuries in the business of designing sailing ships and fishing boats, line the shelves of the oakwood breakfront and mahogany table tops.

David concentrates on the crystal in his hand. Its aura visibly pulsates with a white hot energy. He closes his hand tightly around the Singer and his face wears a determined look. He can't – he won't – let his father lose everything now.

"I'll find a way, Dad. If it's the last thing I do, I'll find a way for you and for Sally."

A sudden, sharp buzzing sound makes David grab his right ear. He pulls out the small hearing aid and shakes the noise out of his head.

Two

David moves with determined strides through the halls of Fischbacher Shipping, Inc., prepared for a confrontation. He stops momentarily outside the glass partition that surrounds the drafting studio. Isaac is working diligently, as usual, and does not see his son. David can't help but think his father looks even more distressed than he did yesterday.

On a mission, David proceeds to the suite of administrative offices and swings the door open wide. Startled at first, Fischbacher's assistant, Janice Cole, rises up behind her desk, almost regally. When she realizes it is David, her expression softens.

"Well, hello, David. What brings you here?" Janice's ivory skin is flawless, even without a touch of makeup. Hanging on the wall over her head, like a deity's image, is a portrait of Nathan Fischbacher, a striking middle-aged man with cold, unfriendly eyes. It's an ironic contrast to Janice's warm-eyed demeanor.

"I'm here to see Fischbacher. I have something important to discuss with him."

Janice registers surprise at David's harsh tone, but remains cordial. "I'm sorry, he's very busy today. But I'll make an appointment –"

"No. This can't wait." David storms past Janice and throws open the door to Fischbacher's private office. Janice moves swiftly to stop him, but David is too quick.

"I'm sorry, Nathan, he just barged right in."

"It's all right, Janice. I'll handle this." Fischbacher's steely expression makes David think the portrait of him was actually flattering. *How could this man's insidious quality ever be captured on canvas?*

Fischbacher's office is decorated even more elaborately than Janice's. But where hers is elegant and tasteful, his is ostentatious and bold, like the man himself. Bronze and marble sculptures, huge seascapes and exotic artifacts collected from his globe-trotting surround him. He wears the expensive Italian-made white suit, red silk tie and handkerchief like a uniform of his elite social status.

"I don't have time for you right now, Nickerson," Fischbacher says, brusquely.

"Too busy selling your company out from under the employees?" David moves strategically in front of Fischbacher, positioning himself to read the man's lips. This irks Fischbacher even more.

"That's none of your business. Now why don't you be a good little boy, run along home, and stay out of grownup affairs."

"Anything that affects my father and sister is my affair," David says, adamantly. "I'll do anything to keep them from being cheated by 'grownups' like you."

Fischbacher sneers. "And just what do you think you can do about it?"

"I can go to the new owners of the company and tell them to keep my father on. He's the best draftsman in the business and you know it. You've seen his blueprints."

Fischbacher feigns indifference. "Blueprints? For what?"

"For the trimmest, fastest, most powerful fleet of cargo ships ever designed. I'm sure they'd be interested, even if you aren't."

"You're father never showed me any such blueprints."

David laughs cynically at the man's gall. "That's a lie and you know it. Dad gave you a full set of those plans."

"Oh, yes," Fischbacher pretends to search his memory. "I seem to recall. Very nice. But worthless at this point. At the end of the month I'll be completely out of the shipping business."

"Then you won't mind if I contact the new owners. I guarantee you they'll feel differently."

Fischbacher makes a point of speaking head on to David.

"Well, Nickerson, I doubt you'll have any luck. This sale is a blind investment. No names are listed on the sale agreement." His smirk says *Ha. Gotcha.*

David is taken aback. He thought surely the sale was public record. He glares at Fischbacher a moment, then, poking his finger in the air defiantly he promises, "I'll find them. And when I do I'll let them know what a cold-hearted monster you really are."

David storms out. Janice steps back quickly out of his way. She follows him tentatively to the outer office, where David abruptly spins and faces her.

"How could you even think of marrying him? How could you give up your whole life, your own dreams, for someone so cruel and heartless?"

Janice is stunned by David's attack. "I don't think I have to justify my decisions to you..."

"Your family helped to build this town, Janice, and helped to make Fischbacher rich and powerful. Then he squeezed the life out of them, forcing them out of their own business."

"He didn't force them out, exactly. He just bought a major share of the stocks -" Janice pauses, aware her defense of Nathan is a lame one.

"Strictly business, right, Janice? Like now? Selling his employees out?"

"You don't understand..."

David grabs her hand and refers to the 20-carat diamond ring she wears. "I understand perfectly. Very impressive ring, Janice." She pulls her hand away. "Just like Nathan Fischbacher – cold and hard. And you're becoming just like him."

David opens the door to leave, then pauses to force home another point. "My Aunt Dorothy is right. All the wrong people have the power. Too bad they don't know what to do with it."

David slams the door behind him. Janice jumps at the force of it. She takes a moment to compose herself, running a nervous hand over the collar of her chic linen suit, then enters Nathan's office.

"Did that troublemaking upstart finally leave?" Fischbacher does not even look up from the pile of financial spreadsheets that cover his desk.

"Yes, he's gone." Janice stands there assessing Nathan.

"Well, what is it?" he snaps impatiently, finally looking up at her.

"About the blueprints – Isaac's designs."

"What about them?"

"They were magnificent. You said so yourself."

"So I did."

"What are you going to do with them?"

Fischbacher casts her an *are you naive?* look. "Sell them, of course, to the highest bidder."

"But you can't do that! They don't belong to you."

"Nickerson designed those plans while he was working for me, so they belong to me as work-for-hire."

"I can't believe you would do this. It's not right."

The surprise and disgust in Janice's eyes cause Fischbacher to move from behind his desk and stand by her. He places his hands patronizingly on Janice's shoulders and speaks in his most charming tone.

"Now, Jan, don't get upset. This is strictly business. As soon as we're married you won't have to concern yourself with any of these little details. Let me make a quick phone call and then I'll take you to your favorite place for a nice, leisurely lunch. Just the two of us."

Janice appears mesmerized by his smoldering gaze. Demurely, she smoothes back a wisp of her jet black hair, which is neatly coifed in a fashionable twist at the nape of her neck. Nathan kisses her lightly, then coaxes her out the door. Janice returns to her desk and sinks into her chair. But then she notices Nathan's extension button is lit up on the phone. Timidly, she presses it down and carefully lifts the receiver to listen.

Fischbacher's tone is low, but commanding. "Remember what I said. Don't let that snoopy kid find *anything*, not one shred of evidence. Is that clear?"

The man on the other end of the phone reassures him. "Have I let you down yet? Don't worry about a thing. I've already set up a bogus file for this sale. No one will ever know who is buying your company."

"And if anyone did find out what was going on, not only would I go to jail, but you'd be occupying the cell next to mine," Fischbacher warns him.

Fischbacher hangs up the phone and Janice quickly replaces the receiver, visibly shaken by this conversation. She fingers her diamond engagement ring, turning it back and forth, back and forth on her finger.

* * *

In the City Administrator's office, David stands at the service counter sifting through a file of legal papers. He is disappointed that the information he hoped to find is not there. *Is it legal to conduct business this way?*

"This can't be the whole file," David protests, pounding the counter. "The names of the buyers aren't listed anywhere, or the date of the sale."

Harry Judd is a snarly little man with a condescending attitude, and David's intense staring at his lips so he can read them makes Judd even more belligerent. "I told you this was a very discreet sale."

"I'll contact Fischbacher's attorney. He can tell me what's going on."

"I doubt it, young man. Lawyer-client confidentiality and all that. I'm sorry," Judd says, not expressing any sorrow at all.

"Yeah. Me, too. But I'm not giving up yet. I'll be back."

Judd shrugs impassively, and David walks away more frustrated than ever. Once David is out of sight, however, Judd places the bogus file that David had examined back in the top drawer of the filing cabinet. From the bottom basket on his own desk he retrieves another file, one marked "Fischbacher Shipping: Sale," and places it in his private desk drawer. He locks the drawer and tucks the key in his vest pocket.

* * *

Bemused, Isaac Nickerson watches the setting sun tint the sky with red and purple ribbons of twilight. He swings idly back and forth on the glider in the same tranquil rhythm of the ocean waves as they ebb and flow on the beach. David opens the screen door and joins his father on the front porch. He sits on the top step and leans comfortably against the railing.

"Nice night, isn't it, Dad?"

"This was your mother's favorite time of day." Isaac's eyes squint to peer into the distant tunnel of a painful memory. "It was twilight when she died. A strange irony, isn't it?"

Isaac signs a heartfelt expression and David's heart lurches. "I miss her, too, Dad." He looks up at the brass mariner's bell hanging in the porch's archway. It could use a polishing, he thinks. That was his mother's favorite task. The bell had come from a ship her grandfather built and her father had sailed around the world more than once. As she polished it to a gleaming finish, she would reminisce about all the exciting adventures her father had had on the high seas. Then she could pretend he was still alive, rocking in his favorite chair by the crackling glow of the fireplace.

"You don't' believe anymore, do you, Dad?"

Isaac snaps out of his reverie. "Believe? Believe in what, Son?"

"Dreams, miracles…"

Isaac is silent a moment, contemplating. "Not the way I used to, David. Maybe not at all. Dreams are only wishful thinking and miracles are accidents. They don't always happen to the most deserving."

David hesitates a moment, then cautiously changes the subject. "I know about Fischbacher selling the company, and about you losing your job. I went to see Fischbacher today."

Isaac stops swinging. "You did?" There was no reaction for David to read.

"I was so mad, Dad, I had to do something. I told him what a rotten stinking thing he was doing to you and everybody in the company. I felt like punching him in the nose."

"That thought occurred to me, too, more than once," a thought that brings a slight smile to Isaac's face.

"What really ticked me off," David continues, his voice rising in agitation, "was his attitude about your blueprints."

Now Isaac frowns. Is it his angry frown, David wonders?

"Which blueprints?"

David forces enthusiasm. "You know, Dad, the ones for the laser-powered cargo ships. He told me they were worthless but I told him I would take them to the new owners of the company, and when they saw your great ideas they'd keep you on."

Isaac shakes his head.

He's dismissing me again, David thinks.

"It's all water under the damn, David. It doesn't matter anymore. I don't even think I'd care to work for the new owners, no matter what they offered me."

"You can't give up now, Dad. Don't you want to see Sally walk again?"

"Yes, of course, but…David, I'm afraid I have a confession." Isaac pauses. The words don't come easily. "There's a part of me, a very selfish part, that doesn't want her to have that operation."

"Why, Dad? I don't understand."

"Because I'm afraid. The operation is dangerous. Sally could die. And if she died, it would be my fault. I killed your mother. I couldn't bear it if I killed Sally, too." Isaac swallows hard, fighting back the tears that want desperately to flow.

"No! That's not true! The crash was an accident. There was so much fog…you just didn't see the turn."

"I should have known better than to drive that road in the fog late at night," Isaac admonishes himself. "But I had to get home. I had to finish my designs for Fischbacher that night. Those damn blueprints you think are so wonderful! They're the reason your mother died. For a lousy set of blueprints." The tears come now, in silent, angry streams, unstoppable.

The lump in David's throat threatens to implode, but he breathes deep and swallows it back down. He rises unsteadily from the step and sits next to his father on the glider. He says nothing, then begins to swing slowly, as though to comfort his father with the gentle rhythm. Isaac collects himself, wipes his eyes with his fingers, and clears his throat self-consciously.

"Now I know why you've never really recovered from the accident," David says, softly. "You've never forgiven yourself."

"And I never will."

Three

On the uppermost level of the Prism Palace, a ferocious rumbling is heard, the growls of an inhuman being suffering great agitation. His blood-red eyes, wide and wild, peer through a small, round window in the wall.

In the adjoining chamber, Saliana stares forlornly out the window of the palace tower. Mindlessly, she runs her fingers through golden hair that cascades over her shoulders and arms, almost touching the floor. She stirs slightly at the beast's presence, aware he is watching her through the opening, but she does not turn in his direction. With her gaze still fixed longingly on the outside world, Saliana picks up her small harp and begins to pluck it. She sings sweetly, but her heart is heavy.

"I know a place where the Moon Spirits play,

Where cathedrals of light form a stairway to heaven.

Deep in the shadows, they hide from the morning

And peek with delight through the cloud covered sky…"

As she sings, the beast's massive, scaly tail swishes and swings, thudding and rattling as it moves. Its growling subsides.

Down in the palace's great temple, musicians tap out a hypnotic rhythm with their hand-held bells and drums. Thus, the choir is cued to begin its droning ceremonial chants. Then, one by one, the subjects climb twelve massive crystalline steps to the Altar of Initiation, where they will come face to face with the High Priestess Jaycina and their inescapable destiny.

Jaycina's robe is the same scarlet red as her lips, which seem always curled, ever so slightly, in a furtive smile. As she stands imperiously at the altar waiting for the fateful initiation to begin, she scans the subjects with a condescending eye. They are blind to their ignorance, fools for a cause they believe to be righteous. And so, she has won yet another victory in her scheme of unrelenting victories. The Glass Snake will be pleased.

Jaycina holds her scepter high in the air and the music and chanting cease abruptly. She turns to the altar and bows in homage to the Serpent Ruler, whose image glares at her with eyes as deadly cold as the black onyx from which they are cast. She sets the scepter upright in its niche, then turns to face the subjects again.

"From this day forward, you will bow only to him, live your life only for him, worship the power and reflect in the glory that is his and his alone." As Jaycina pontificates dramatically, her ceremonial headdress of solid gold, diamonds, and rubies glitters atop her high-swept ebony hair, providing a breathtaking contrast to the stark white interior of the temple.

The High Priestess extends her hand toward the first subject, and the music and chanting resume. The subject offers her his personal crystal, a large hexagonal emerald, which Jaycina places in a holographic console. An intense surge of electrical energy is heard and a glow of light emanates from the console for a few seconds.

Jaycina removes the crystal from the console and returns it to the subject. As she speaks to him, her eyes are a penetrating force, and his face glows with the expected fulfillment of her promises. No longer is the subject a free entity, empowered by his own free will, but he has yet to discover that this ceremony is the precursor to his enslavement.

"Your allegiance to the great Serpent Ruler of the Prism Palace has been recorded in the Crystal Chamber of Records, an allegiance which must never falter in this lifetime or through an eternity of lifetimes."

The subject bows to her, kisses the elaborate diamond ring on her finger, then walks across the altar and out of sight. Another subject steps up to take his place, and the ritual is repeated again and again, until the dozens of men and women standing in wait on the crystalline steps have been indoctrinated and purified.

Outside, darkness looms, eclipsing the sun, the moon, and the stars. The only visible light emanates from the Prism Palace, but it lends an eerie, foreboding contrast to the blackness that pervades the Island.

In the tunnels beneath the palace, hundreds of men toil in the mines, extracting crystals and gemstones from the rocky earth. Glass lanterns provide an uneven, yellow illumination. The heat is unbearable, and some of the men falter from a lack of oxygen.

As the stones are chipped away, they are piled onto a cart. When the cart is filled, a worker pushes it to the end of the mineshaft where the slave master examines each sample and places it in a bucket. The bucket is lowered by a long rope into an underground well to cleanse the stones. When the bucket rises, the stones are clean and sparkle in their raw, natural beauty.

Inside his hideaway cave dwelling, Ishtar stares intently into the flickering light of the campfire. He would jump into the flames and disintegrate into ashes if it would solve

his dilemma. He rubs his eyes and runs a weary hand over his beard. Dorinda offers him a drink, but Ishtar just waves it away.

"You cannot blame yourself, Ishtar," Dorinda tries to console him. "You thought you were helping our people, but you were deceived, too, by Jaycina's lies."

"I cannot believe she would betray us," Ishtar he says angrily. "She let me use my skills, my knowledge to design the Temple. I provided the bio-magnetic codes for the Crystal Chamber and literally condemned the Islanders to a life of slavery and hope-lessness. How could I have been so blind?"

"What you did, you did in good faith, Ishtar."

Ishtar bolts upright and paces back and forth in torment. "Tell that to Saliana, to my daughter, imprisoned by that hideous – that hideous thing they call our ruler, our god. How can Saliana ever forgive me for what I've done?" Ishtar buries his face in his hands, artistic hands that have brought to life the dream of a divine spirit. Now the dream has been corrupted.

Dorinda stands beside her dear friend. "Saliana knows that you would never have deliberately brought her to harm. She trusts and loves you now as she did when she accompanied you to the palace. You cannot break under this pain you bear. You must be strong, to find a way to help her."

Ishtar picks up his tools, those of a craftsman who works with metals and gemstones. "How, Dorinda? With these?" He shakes the primitive implements angrily in the air. "They are outmoded and useless without the stones and minerals that once flourished on this side of the Island. I have barely enough crystal to make a trinket. He has all of it. That monster. He has all the power now. He is invincible." Ishtar tosses the tools onto his worktable in disgust. "And now, with Saliana's music, he will also be im-mortal."

Dorinda grips Ishtar's arm. "No. We must not let that happen. We must find someone to help us."

"But who, Dorinda? There is no one left but you and I, and Judiah. The others are too weak or too sick to be of any use."

"It must be someone not from the Island, but someone who does share your knowledge and your courage. He will rescue Saliana and destroy the Glass Snake."

Ishtar is skeptical, but curious. "How will you find such as soul? And how can you possibly entice him to come here at the risk of his own life?"

"He will come, Ishtar," Dorinda promises, "to save a life that means more to him than his own."

Four

Port Avalon, first day of Summer

David pulls on a thin rope, hoists a small wire basket out of the water and climbs down the ladder of the pier. He crouches down on the beach, removes the twelve crystals from the basket one by one, then places them carefully on the wet, hard sand. David looks heavenward for a moment. The sun is high and hot, its glare pure white, a symbol of the cosmic light energy. The sky is a startling blue and, under the sun's dazzling rays, the water below is a smooth mirror, a deep green sea of glass that extends unto infinity. David turns his attention back to the crystals and begins to arrange them in a circle.

Sally maneuvers her wheelchair along the pier and down a specially built ramp that allows her to come down to the beach next to him.

David looks up to see her. "Hi, Sally. I didn't know you were there."

"What are you doing with your crystals?"

"I just gave them a good overnight cleansing and I want them to sit out in the sun awhile."

Sally shares David's fascination with the "magic rocks," more out of adoration for her older brother than an affinity for the crystals themselves. When otosclerosis made him deaf at age seven, he withstood the pain, the surgeries and the disappointment with such courage that even five-year-old Sally was deeply moved. He never told the creepy kids at school how well he could read the cruel remarks on their lips. He worked diligently to keep up his normal speech, but also learned to sign expertly, even teaching Sally so they could tell private little jokes to each other. At least he could feel the pulse of music and the powerful rhythm of the pounding surf with his hearing aid. And maybe, Sally had insisted to her parents, David really could hear things that hearing people could not.

"Why are you doing that?"

"I've been working with them quite a lot lately and they need to be reenergized," David explains. "If we could get a good electrical storm, they'd really be good and strong again, and I could study their individual molecular structure and vibrational patterns better."

"Tell me about them again, David, where they came from and what their powers are."

"Okay." David knows Sally prefers the mystical legends to all that science stuff about atoms, neutrons, and protons. So he plays these sessions with his sister up to the hilt by giving her the most imaginative descriptions he can conjure up. He sits down comfortably on the sand, then holds up a deep violet-colored quartz crystal.

"This one is an amethyst," David begins. "It was used in ancient cultures as an amulet to prevent drunkenness. The people got stoned instead."

Sally's corn silk blonde ponytail bobs perkily atop her head when she throws it back and laughs.

"Actually" - David is serious now - "it's a wonderful meditation stone that brings responses from your spiritual guides when you are troubled about something in your life." David puts the amethyst down and selects another stone, a deep blue one.

"The Lapis Lazuli was a favorite of the ancient Egyptians," he lectures, sounding like an archeological guide. "The gold speckles on it aren't really gold, but pyrite – fools gold. The Egyptians used it to call upon the great wisdom of their ancestors when making major decisions about their families, like should they let their mother-in-law live with them, or drown old 'Mummy' in the Nile."

Sally laughs even harder now, and claps her hands.

David picks up a large opaque stone, the vibrant color of emerald green meadows. "The malachite is a great one for men. It can make a mighty warrior out of a timid mouse, or a Prince Charming out of a complete nerd."

"Like you!" Sally teases him.

David reaches up and yanks on her ponytail affectionately.

"Show me the rose crystal, David. The pretty pink one. It's my favorite."

"It's beautiful, isn't it?" David holds a deep rose-colored crystal. "It works on the frequency of faith and unconditional love." He signs the word *love*, and gives the crystal to Sally to hold. "I'm going to have this set in a pendant for you to wear next to your heart. That's where it really belongs."

Sally's eyes mist over and she, too, signs as she whispers, "Oh, David, I love you, too." But when she sees the Singer, she squeals with delight. "David! Let me see that one."

David holds up the Singer so she can see it from every angle. "Isn't it excellent?"

Sally is almost breathless. "It looks just like a sailing ship! I've never seen anything like it!"

"There isn't another like it in the whole world," David boasts. "It's called a Singer because its vibrations sing all the mysteries of the universe. At least that's what Aunt Dorothy said. I call it my Crystal Clipper," he says and signs, "a ship to take me to far off, magical places – with the help of my imagination, of course."

"Oh, David, wouldn't it be wonderful if you could sail off to a magical place where all your dreams could come true?"

"And if I did, I'd take you with me, Sally, to a place where you would walk and dance and be happy again." He spins her wheelchair a few turns.

"And where you could hear again," Sally adds, as though the dream just might be possible. "So, if we're going to sail off on a Crystal Clipper, hadn't you better get your magic rocks all re-energized? It looks like it's going to rain any minute."

David looks up, surprised to see that dark clouds are beginning to appear. "Aye, Captain. You're right. A good electrical storm will do the trick all right. This might be a good time to try that new energy formation I just read about." He picks up a small twig and draws a pyramid shape in the sand. Then he draws an inverted pyramid over the other pattern, creating a six-pointed Star of David.

Sally crinkles her nose. "What's an energy formation?"

"They're really called gridwork patterns. I don't know much about them yet, but this double pyramid is supposed to be very powerful, for something. I'll have to read up on it more."

"David, do you think you should experiment with it yet? Something awful could happen."

But David is oblivious to her concern. Already he is placing a crystal strategically on each point of the star, with the Singer at the apex of the pyramid. Just as he completes the grid pattern, a crackling bolt of lightning streaks across the sky, skitters along the surface of the water, and strikes the Singer full on. Acting as a conduit of energy, the Singer transmits the lightning to every crystal in the grid, emblazoning the sand in a kaleidoscopic fury. The force throws David over on his back and knocks him out cold.

Five

When David regains consciousness, the storm has passed and a hazy mist of filtered sunlight spreads out over the coastline. He shakes his head to revive himself, then lets out a low whistle, amazed at the shock he just experienced. The crystals sparkle vibrantly in the sand, humming audibly with electro-magnetic energy. David holds his hand just inches above them to feel their hot pulse. He is dumbfounded, but ecstatic.

"Holy cow! Sally, take a look at this! Sally..." David turns to look at her but she is not there. All that remains is her empty wheel chair. David is apprehensive, then frantic as he calls for her.

"Sally! Sally, where are you! Are you all right?"

David stands there helplessly, looking up to the pier and back down again, turning around in the sand, looking in the other direction. He can't believe she has disappeared. But how? Quickly, he retrieves his crystals and wraps them in their silk pouch, which he fastens to his belt. He races up the ramp of the pier calling his sister's name. He runs to the far end of the pier where a few small boats are moored, but sees no signs of Sally or anyone else.

Then, coming from out of nowhere, a startling ball of light dances in mid-air, stopping David in his tracks. A sound emanates from the light, the most beautiful sound – the *first* pure sound - he has heard in years. Whose sweet voice is that singing? David believes it must be an angel, for who (or what) else would sing of cathedrals of light and stairways to heaven in a voice so sublime it defies description. He walks apprehensively toward it, still softly calling his sister's name. David's heart nearly pounds out of his chest when an apparition appears, a holographic image of a mysterious Gypsy woman peering into a crystal ball.

"Come closer, David," the Gypsy invites him. Hesitant, David walks closer to the image, amazed that he can hear her voice. It has a reverberant quality, but he can make out her words distinctly. He touches his ear to check his hearing aid. It's still there.

"Your Sally is here, in my crystal ball, but far away in a strange and dangerous place. You will find her when you have journeyed from the darkness to the light. But you must take the first step, unafraid."

David peers into the gypsy's clear globe but sees nothing. As suddenly as it appeared, the hologram dissolves, and the mist separates like a curtain drawn open to reveal a breathtaking wonder. "Holy cow!" he cries, then gives out that same low whistle of amazement.

A magnificent, gleaming white sailing ship, sleek as satin, is anchored by the wharf. Her awesome masts jut proudly into the air, with a cumulous burst of sail filling the skyline. The gangplank is down, inviting David aboard. He strides swiftly up to her main deck and takes in the unbelievable beauty of her. From stem to stern, she is pure white, from the polished wood of her decks to the tautly woven silk of her sails. Eagerly, David runs up and down the main deck looking for someone on board.

"Hello! Is anyone here? Hello!"

The ship lurches forward suddenly. The gangplank mysteriously rises and secures itself to the rails, leaving David with no way off. The sails puff up and pick up the strong westerly wind, and the clipper casts off from the dock to the open seas.

"Wait! Where are we going? What's happening?"

But no one answers. David is all alone on this mystical clipper ship, now sailing under its own power, with no captain or crew, destination unknown. And sail she does, swift and smooth. From the rail of her goblet-shaped stern, David watches the coastline of his hometown become a distant image.

In a surprising turn, David's fear subsides. He is now curiously amenable to this adventure, and decides to inspect the ship. Slowly, he makes his way, touching every piece of equipment, running his hands along the rails and rigs of the clipper's expertly constructed body.

"That's strange," he remarks, touching the mizzenmast. "It's cold, like marble or stone, not wood."

In fact, all three of the ship's huge masts are smooth and translucent. Shiny gold rings woven with links as supple as a necklace chain encircle the masts at their bases, with the mizzenmast wearing several rings from bottom to top.

"Gold rings. What could they be for?"

David makes his way down the ladder of the main deck to the Captain's quarters and looks for some signs of life. There is a bunk and a desk, but the cabin is devoid of

any personal items except for a journal that lies closed on top of the desk. David picks up the leather-bound, hand-tooled book and reads the cover inscription aloud.

"Captain's Log - The Great Ship Moon Singer."

He opens the cover and reads the handwritten entry:

"Spanning the water at 200 feet from stem to stern, she boasts 20,000 square feet of sails, woven from pure silk skein. Her mizzenmast towers 150 feet high, sculpted from pure quartz crystal. The rings of gold are power generators, allowing her to travel faster than the speed of light. Christened and set to sea on this 21st day of June... *why, that's today!...*

Log recorded by Captain David Nickerson..."

Astonished, David drops the book as though it is possessed, and jumps back away. But once again curiosity overcomes his fear. He retrieves the book, then frantically turns the pages only to find them completely blank. He sinks into the captain's chair, shaken by this discovery. It was all too much for him to fathom.

"This has got to be a dream. This can't be real. I've been working with those damn crystals so much they've invaded my sleep." He reads his name again.

"Captain David Nickerson." He laughs at the incredibility of it. "Well, Sally, you wanted me to sail on a crystal clipper, and you got your wish. The Moon Singer no less."

David wanders back up to the main deck and stands at the helm, as though he truly is the captain of his own ship. The dazzling brightness of the sun forms a cathedral of light through billowy clouds, and the Moon Singer shimmers like a diamond atop the water. Together they sail across the magnificent blue-green seascape, covering mile after endless mile of sparkling ocean. There was nothing for David to do but to go along, to let the "dream" play out to its conclusion. Then, perhaps, it would all make sense.

Six

The clipper's towering rigging, tuned as tightly as a violin, thrums a monotonous song as it sways in the brisk wind. A sudden lurch of the ship startles David awake and he almost falls off the bench he is sleeping on. Another lurch and David is on his feet, trying to balance himself as the ship sways with the increasing speed and power of the wind.

A violent thunderstorm rolls in and the sky becomes black and foreboding. Building up into a hill of water, the sea lifts the Moon Singer up by the stern and sends her crashing down hard. Giant waves topple forward, with wind batting off their crests, and sweep across the main deck in a flooding carpet of water. David is knocked off his feet and sent sliding across the width of the deck. Desperate, he grabs onto anything he can find to keep from being washed overboard. On his hands and knees, on his belly, anyway he can, David makes his way to the helm, grabs onto a pile of rope and ties himself down.

The gale force winds howl like a banshee warning that death is imminent, and David shudders inside and out with terror. The clipper dips her yardarms deep into the water, then shoots them high above the surface as she sways and rolls to the cross seas. Time after time, the phosphorescent surf explodes over David's head and he gasps desperately for air, coughing water up from his lungs.

As a final assault, a mountain of water moves under the clipper, lifting her higher and higher to its peak. But there she sits, in suspended animation, the wind a haunting siren's song, when once again the hologram appears.

"You are at the crossroads, and the choice is yours, David Nickerson. Do you step backward in fear, or forward in courage? Either way, the fate of your Sally is in your hands."

"Who are you!" David screams at her. "Where are you taking me? I don't understand any of this."

"There is no time to question," the Gypsy urges him. "Make your choice before the spell is broken and Sally is lost forever."

David is more angry than frightened. His dream voyage has become a nightmare, and the Gypsy is playing games with Sally's life. He has no choice but to play along if he is ever to see her again.

"All right! All right! Take me to Sally, damn you!" With David's decision as its driving force, the Moon Singer picks up incredible speed, pinning David harder against the helm. Her motion is smooth and swift as she moves on the peak of a huge wave, soaring higher and higher, ascending from the surface of the water and taking astral flight. Through galaxies and billions of stars she travels, faster than the speed of light. Then, breaking the barriers of time and space, riding a cosmic river of diamonds and pearls, the clipper floats free and gentle toward the moon.

Oblivious to his fear, David loses himself in the splendor of the moment. Such indescribable, unearthly beauty, such inexplicable joy, such infinite peace and serenity.

Feeling that the storm has passed, David unties himself and finds his sea legs. He makes his way to the clipper's stern, and steadies himself at the rail. Oddly, trailing behind the ship is not an ocean of calm water, but a sea of glass, slick as a glacier. Through this looking glass of illusion, David watches the panoramic landscape of his home, his town, the earth, his past – as they fade into the distance, and then away completely.

* * *

The moon is high and silvery, creating a silhouette of the Island that lies in the distance, as the Moon Singer drifts toward land. She comes to a halt a few hundred yards from the shore and, under her own power, she drops anchor. A small dinghy is lowered with David inside, and when it hits the water David rows to shore. He jumps from the dinghy into the shallow water, then pulls the boat onto the beach, mooring it in the sand. Just then a huge cloud moves across the moon, eclipsing it completely, leaving David in total darkness.

"Oh, great. I can't see a thing now. Where's a flashlight when you need one?"

David's offhandedness does nothing to relieve the squeezing in his gut. Then, in an unexpected flash of light, the Gypsy's image reappears. Startled, David falls backward onto the sand with a thud.

"Before you can walk easily in the light, you must become accustomed to no light at all," the Gypsy says sprightly.

"I'm kind of getting that impression. But do you have to speak in cryptic messages? It would be *really* helpful if you just told me what was going on in plain English." He stands up and brushes the sand from his clothes.

"The message changes for each who hears. Just as the road bends differently for each who ventures forth."

"Thanks. That makes a lot more sense," David sneers. "Okay, for Sally's sake I'll play along with your little game. Just tell me which way to go here…"

"It's not where you go that matters. It's where you *are*," the Gypsy says liltingly, obviously taking pleasure in her own riddles. Then, she begins to fade away.

"Hey! Wait! Wherever I am, how come I can hear you?" David moves toward the fading image, but the hologram disappears, and David is in complete darkness once again.

"It's not where you go, it's where you are," he mumbles to himself. "I wish I knew where I *are*."

David walks away from the beach and into the density of the Island. Night creatures make eerie sounds. Twigs crackle under his feet. Something swats him in the face. "Ouch!"

He trips over a rock. "Ouch!"

David moves further along with only a few inches of visibility before him and begins to breathe heavily, fear of the unknown rising within him. Then, as though the ground has opened up and swallowed him, David falls screaming into a deep narrow hole, banging and scraping his body on its rocky sides all the way to the bottom.

Seven

A stunned and barely conscious David lies at the entryway to Ishtar's cave. Carefully, Ishtar moves the boy closer to the light of the campfire. He checks David's eyes, his respiration, and his wrist pulse for signs of life. Satisfied that he is alive, his attention shifts to the silk pouch David carries tied to his belt.

"Well, well. What have we here?" Ishtar removes the pouch from David's belt and pours the contents into his hand. Surprise and pleasure register as one emotion on Ishtar's face as the colored crystals fill his palm. His reaction then evolves to ecstasy at the sight of the Singer crystal, and then to bewilderment.

David stirs, moans in pain, then falls unconscious again. Ishtar selects a few of the colored crystals and, with his cutter's tools, skillfully chips a few pieces off each one. Among the twelve crystals that David carries, there are all the colors of the body chakras: red, gold, yellow, green, blue, indigo and violet. They will coordinate and harmonize David's body with etheric forces to bring about healing, wholeness and spiritual unfoldment.

Ishtar places the pieces in a copper bowl, then respectfully returns the rest of the crystals to David's pouch. First, boiling water is poured over the crystal fragments, then a small energy pyramid made of copper wire is placed over the bowl. In a short while, the water is heated and imbued with the energy and power of the crystals. When David stirs, almost regaining consciousness, Ishtar offers him a taste of the elixir from a cup. David coughs and sputters and the brew dribbles from his lips.

"I know it's wretched," Ishtar says flatly, "but it will help to heal you quickly. Drink up." David drinks a little, then tries to move, groaning loudly at the attempt. "Be still," Ishtar says, soothingly. "Let the elixir do its work. Sleep awhile."

Each time David stirs from his sleep to a semi-conscious state, Ishtar offers him a taste of the medicinal brew. Hours later, David awakes fully.

"Where am I? What happened?"

Ishtar helps David to sit up a bit, propping him up with some cushions. "You had a very bad fall, but I don't believe anything is broken."

"It feels like *everything* is broken." David takes a bleary-eyed look around, then sets his gaze on Ishtar, puzzled. The man is bearded, distinguished, with warm yet penetrating eyes. *His clothes. What is it about his clothes? They are almost medieval. Did I take a quantum leap backward in time?* "What is this place?" David asks.

"This is my camp, and my humble home these days. You made a rather grand entrance, falling down that hole as you did."

Ishtar's voice is rich and resonant, his tone cordial. Music to David's ears. David is astounded that he can hear the man speak, just as he heard the Gypsy. "I couldn't see a thing. It was pitch dark up there." He stops a beat, weary, then, "Exactly what is up there? Some sort of island?"

"Yes, you are correct."

"Where is it? I mean, what part of the world am I in?"

"More to the point, from what world have you come?

"The States," David replies matter-of-factly. Ishtar looks at David blankly. "United," David qualifies. "…of America? Earth?"

Now Ishtar nods in recognition. "A long journey. What brought you to our island?"

"A sailing ship brought me here but, believe me, I still don't really know how I got here."

"I don't understand."

"Well, first I'm on the beach by my house," David begins his story, "cleaning my crystals -"

"You work with crystals?" Ishtar jumps in.

"Yes, now and then. Well, I laid them all out on the sand. I wanted them to be out in the electrical storm that was coming -"

"Yes. Very good for them."

"...I started arranging them in patterns. You know - grid patterns?"

Ishtar nods. "I am familiar with such things."

"When I arranged them in a Star of David -"

Ishtar is further intrigued. "A most powerful grid."

"I'll say. When that lightning bolt hit the Singer -"

Ishtar's left eyebrow shoots upward. "Singer?"

"Yes, a crystal my aunt gave me." David opens his pouch and presents the Singer to Ishtar. "Amazing, isn't it?"

"Amazing." Ishtar's quiet affirmation belies the fact that he has already seen, and recognized, the sacred Record Keeper.

"The lightning strike hit the Singer head on and the force knocked me out cold."

"Unconscious? How long?" Ishtar presses David's eyelids back to study his pupils for signs of a concussion.

"I'm not sure, really. But when I looked around for Sally -"

"Sally?"

"My sister, Sally. She was gone and her wheel chair was empty."

"Your Sally cannot walk." Ishtar's tone is sympathetic.

"No, she was in a car accident. And that's what makes it even crazier. I mean, where could she go? I ran around looking for her everywhere and that's when I saw it - a ghost or an image, like a hologram. It was some Gypsy woman telling me Sally was in her crystal ball, in some far off, dangerous place. She said I would find her only when I could take the journey from the darkness to the light. Weird, huh?"

Just then, Dorinda enters the cave and moves about in the shadows. She lights the candles on a candelabra, illuminating the volumes of books and artisan's tools on Ishtar's worktable.

"Who's that?" David whispers, straining to sit up to see her better.

"Don't be alarmed. It's only Dorinda, a very good friend." Ishtar's hands on David's shoulders settle him back on the pillows. "Perhaps you should sleep now."

David draws in a shallow breath. He is still very weary, but eager to continue with his story.

"There's more. It's even more incredible. This big white ship suddenly appears, an old time ship - a clipper - I couldn't believe my eyes. But there was not a soul on it, no one to sail it. It began to move, with me on it, and I thought, well, why not? If this was all a dream or something, maybe I should see it through to the end. I had to find Sally no matter what."

"And the ship brought you here?"

"Yes, after the worst sea storm I had ever seen in my life. I thought I was going to die, but when the storm was over, we just drifted to the island. Then, on the shore, there she was again."

"The Gypsy."

"Yes, the hologram, coaxing me onto the island with these crazy riddles."

"Riddles. What kind of riddles?" Ishtar hides his amusement with a straight face.

"Cryptic messages like, 'Before you can walk in the light you must get used to no light at all,'" David recounts with a tinge of sarcasm, "and 'It's not where you go that matters, it's where you are.' Stuff like that."

Ishtar stifles the urge to laugh. "Quite profound philosophies."

"Then she disappeared. And it became totally dark, no moon or anything. Then I fell right into a big hole or something. That's the last thing I remember." David holds his head, once again aware of his aches and pains.

"You've been talking too much. Get some more rest now," Ishtar says firmly.

Acquiescent, David settles down into the cushions and tries to get comfortable, but he is startled to see Dorinda's face peering at him over Ishtar's shoulder. David lifts his head to get a better look at her. No turban or dangly earrings, but the face is the same well-worn face. Soft hair, blonde going gray. Her clothes, too, are an eclectic style like Ishtar's. She moves back into the shadows again.

"It's her! David's cry is more a hoarse whisper. "She's back."

"Who? Dorinda?"

"No - yes - I mean - she's the Gypsy, the hologram."

"Well, you know what they say about Gypsy holograms. They all look alike." Ishtar offers David more of the elixir. "Drink this, it will make you sleep peacefully."

David shakes his head, refusing the drink. "No. She knows where Sally is. I've got to talk to her."

"Dorinda has gone about her business now. Tomorrow you can question her," Ishtar promises. Tonight, sleep and regain your strength. Here."

David drinks then closes his eyes, yielding to a deep, sweet sleep. Ishtar slips quietly from the cave and finds Dorinda just outside the entryway.

"Dorinda? What have you been up to now?" Ishtar chastises her. "Did you really entice that boy here with that hologram business, and that silly Gypsy disguise of yours?"

"Yes," Dorinda admits, smugly. "And I did it rather well, didn't I."

"But you know that leaving the parameters of the island is dangerous," Ishtar reminds her sharply. "You could have been suspended somewhere out there in time, or dissipated entirely."

"I had to take the chance, Ishtar. For Saliana. For all of us."

"But how can we be sure the boy is up to the challenge?"

"He has courage, Ishtar. He withstood the most horrifying storm. And he has knowledge of the crystals."

"Yes, he has crystals, including the Record Keeper. But doesn't even know the power of what he possesses, let alone how to use it. And didn't you notice, in his ear, the hearing instrument. The poor boy is deaf. Although I must admit he speaks splendidly well."

"His affliction, dear Ishtar, is more advantage than handicap. He can hear what others cannot, or I never could have connected with him. He heard Saliana's song."

A look of knowing crosses Ishtar's face. "Saliana's song. Of course. And now he can hear everything, everything we say. Because he heard Saliana's song."

"From that moment, he was bound to us by fate."

"Yes, but he is also young and innocent," Ishtar says, still circumspect. "He will be no match for Jaycina's cunning or her ruthlessness."

Obviously undaunted, Dorinda cajoles further. "There is something more that he has, the one thing above all that will make him succeed. He has desire, Ishtar. Desire to find his sister no matter what the cost to himself."

"To find his sister, yes. But not Saliana," Ishtar volleys with her again. "How can you possibly convince him to take up our cause?"

"By making him believe that in rescuing Saliana he will rescue his sister as well."

"I don't know, Dorinda. Deceiving him - it just isn't the right thing to do."

Dorinda speaks the solemn truth. "It is the only thing we *can* do."

Eight

Having slept restfully through the night, David is able to accompany Ishtar to meet a man named Judiah. He follows closely on Ishtar's heels as the older man carries a torch to light their way along a secluded path.

"Why are you using a torch? Don't you have a flashlight?" David asks.

"Flashlights are a thing of the past," Ishtar answers.

"I don't understand," David says, consternation becoming part of his personality.

"You will, in time," Ishtar states flatly.

David is doubtful. This entire experience is something he can't understand, let alone why there is no electrical power on this island, or why Ishtar lives in a cave instead of a house.

"And besides," David presses on, "if it's morning, why is there no sunlight?"

"Our island is devoid of any light at all," Ishtar says, stating the obvious, and gloomy, truth.

"How can that be? No sun? No moon? That's not possible."

"Just as you can hear me speak? On our island, the impossible becomes possible."

"Great. Now you're talking like the Gypsy. In Riddles." David's patience is wearing thin. "Besides, I thought I would be able to talk to Dorinda today, to ask her about Sally."

"Dorinda is an elusive one. I never know when she will appear or disappear."

David sniffs caustically. "You're not the only one."

Ishtar stops short and David nearly piles into him. "We are meeting a friend here," Ishtar says. "He is the only other Islander besides Dorinda and I who has managed to retain his freedom, such as it is. I've asked Judiah to meet us, so we can go and see this sailing ship you speak of."

As his name is mentioned, Judiah approaches, also carrying a torch. He is a mole-like, overly solicitous little man. Usually, he defers to Ishtar's wisdom and authority. Dorinda has often expressed her doubts about Judiah's allegiance, but Ishtar usually dismisses Dorinda's suspicious rantings.

"Ishtar, good. Dorinda said you would be here." Judiah acknowledges David. "Is this the boy?"

"Yes. David Nickerson. He's come to the island under mysterious circumstances. I thought you would want to see the ship."

"Yes. Yes. It just may provide our means of escape," Judiah's voice dances up and down annoyingly. "Can you lead the way, David?"

David tilts his head in a gesture of uncertainty. "It was so dark when I came here. The only thing I remember is the moon was high and full and the island was a silhouette in the sky. Then the moon eclipsed totally and it was pitch black."

"Then you arrived from the west side of the island," Judiah surmises.

"That's good," Ishtar comments. "It means the ship is far from the Palace's view and won't be easy for them to spot."

"For who to spot?"

Ishtar ignores David's question. "There is also a series of torch posts along the beach that we can light without being detected."

"Detected by who?" David wants to know.

"Whom," Ishtar corrects him.

"Okay. Detected by *whom*? I thought you were the only ones on this island."

Ishtar puts him off again. "I'll explain later. Let's proceed to the ship."

At the beach, Ishtar finds a torch post anchored deep in the sand and lights the wick. He finds another and lights it as well. In the amber glow, David spots the dinghy he used to row to shore. It sits securely on a sand bank as though waiting for David's return.

"There. There's the dinghy."

The trio dashes to the boat, pushes it to the shore and into the water, then they jump in one by one. David rows the dinghy to the Moon Singer. Atop the black water, the clipper ship emanates a mystical white glow, as though to light their way in the dark. Ishtar and Judiah are noticeably impressed, especially Ishtar whose face expresses the remembrance of an awesome power.

"Magnificent. Magnificent," Ishtar exclaims.

"Amazing," Judiah agrees, as usual. If his eyes were opened any wider the orbs would fall out. "Truly amazing."

David rows to the side of the ship and ties the dinghy to the rope ladder. One by one, the three men climb the ladder and board the ship.

Once aboard, Ishtar and Judiah find lanterns to light on the ship's deck. They carry the lanterns as they inspect the ship from stem to stern. Ishtar stops at the base of the clipper's mizzenmast and runs his hand up and down the surface. He touches one of the gold rings and inspects it carefully.

"Never would I have thought it possible. Never." Ishtar's voice is almost hushed in reverence.

"What is it, Ishtar?" Judiah asks, replicating Ishtar's tenor.

"Let's go below," Ishtar says, avoiding Judiah's probe.

Down in the captain's quarters, David picks up the leather-bound journal lying on the desk. "This is the Captain's Log. It explains about the ship. I couldn't believe my eyes when I read it."

Ishtar scans the log, then pounds it jubilantly with his fist. "I knew it! Her masts are made of crystal. More pure and more powerful than anything mined on the island. And the rings - they are the impetus for her power. The extraordinary energy from this ship could provide the means to overthrow the Snake."

David's stomach jumps. "The *snake*? What snake?"

"Judiah, we have here more than a means for our escape. We have the weapon to destroy our enemy, to redeem the island as our own once again."

David is really perturbed now. "What enemy? Who are you trying to destroy?"

Now it is Judiah who ignores David's questions. "You may be right, Ishtar. But how do we capture such energy from this ship? You know that all of the island's electrical currents have been diverted to the Palace. We have no conductors, no conduits."

Ishtar reflects a moment. "It will take some doing, perhaps some miracle. But soon the Island of Darkness will exist no more. It will once again be the City of Light, the light of hope for us all."

* * *

Later that day at the entryway to Ishtar's camp, Ishtar gives an apprehensive David instructions as he is about to explore the island alone. He finally agreed with Dorinda that they must use David's determination to find his sister to their own advantage, but his decision is more than a deceptive ploy. Ishtar knows the true power of the Moon Singer and the source of that power; that the Singer is a microcosm of the ship's infinite knowledge and wisdom, for it is a chip from the same vein of crystals from which the Moon Singer's masts have been sculpted.

"I have work to do and cannot go with you to find your Sally," Ishtar says, not revealing the true reason for sending David out by himself. "Judiah has cleared a path for you to walk safely around the island. As long as you carry this lantern, you will find your way easily."

David's hands are as pleading as his eyes. "But, Ishtar, I haven't the faintest idea where I'm going. The only reason I found my way here was because of the Gypsy hologram - or Dorinda. Whoever it is, she's the only one who knows where Sally is. What if she doesn't appear again?"

"She will appear again. There is some very mysterious connection between you. Allow it to reveal itself. Now, if for some reason you become lost, or encounter trouble, come back as quickly as you can. Here." He hands David a small pouch. "Sprinkle these along the path behind you as you walk."

David looks at the granules inside the pouch. "What are they?"

"Seed crystals. Once they touch the earth, they will glow. If you fall into danger or darkness, the seed crystals will lead you back to my camp, but will be extinguished under your feet."

"What if I don't find Sally? What if she isn't out there after all?"

"Then you must keep trying until you do find her," Ishtar encourages him. "Now, go. May God be with you."

Cautiously, David maneuvers his way along the path, holding the lantern in one hand and sprinkling the seed crystals every few yards with the other. Now and then he softly calls his sister's name, and tries to invoke the image of the Gypsy once again.

"Sally. Sally, are you here? Sally?" *I feel like an idiot. How can she hear me anyway if she's in some crystal ball?* "Gypsy? Or whatever you are. Where are you? I need some assistance here. Come out, come out wherever you are."

David continues to walk along the path for what seems like miles. He feels tired and sore and decides to rest a moment, but a faint glow in the distance causes him to hasten his step. David calls out apprehensively. "Is that you, Gypsy? Dorinda? Sally?"

Continuing on warily toward the light, David notices the glow intensify. He comes to a clearing and moves decisively toward the radiance, then comes to an abrupt halt, both puzzled and fascinated by what he sees.

Across the valley, on the summit of a hill, lies the Prism Palace, a shimmering vision amidst an otherwise dark and dense terrain. At first glance, it appears to be a crystal of monolithic proportions. It is deceptively transparent, with near-blinding refractions of light that obscure its interior from view.

Angular and defined, the structure reminds David of a geometric puzzle with smooth and seamless interlocking pieces: a tetragon on the left, a trigonal on the right, a hexagonal center that towers over all. He is compelled to run to its threshold, to let the Celestial rainbows of color wash over him, embrace him, consume him. But his ethereal impulse is jerked back to hard reality when he looks more clearly at the sight before him.

On the perimeter of the Palace grounds is a dormant volcano. A ritual is taking place at its mouth, with hundreds of subjects totally entranced by throbbing chants and the staccato pounding of ceremonial drums. David conceals himself behind a tree and watches, mesmerized.

Attending the ceremony is the High Priestess Jaycina, strikingly costumed in a vibrant ceremonial gown and jeweled headdress. All of the subjects wear their customary simple white robes, except for one of them whose robe is embellished with a breastplate of ornamental metals and gemstones. The subject is led, resistant and writhing, to a pedestal at the edge of the volcano. Immediately, sparks begin to generate from the volcano, as though it is hungry and about to be fed.

At Jaycina's imperial gesture, two guards move a huge lodestone into position at the far side of the volcano, then step aside. Swiftly, an enormous flash of electrical energy surges between the lodestone and the victim's breastplate. He is literally magnetized and lifted high into the air, floating on the electrical current like a puppet on a string. While he hovers over the center of the volcano's mouth, the drumming and chanting built to a mad frenzy. The lodestone is then pushed aside, cutting off the free-floating electrical current.

The victim plunges helplessly into the depths of the volcano, screaming screams that David now wishes he could not hear. The drums and chants crescendo, echoing throughout the valley, vibrating through David's body, then cease when the volcano is appeased.

Heart pounding fiercely, terror reflected in his eyes, David turns to run, but is surprisingly overtaken by two men. As David struggles to fight them off, he drops the lantern, which emblazons the clothing of one of his assailants. The flames flare dangerously close to David's own clothing, but he breaks free.

His feet flying over the seed crystals, David runs back down the path to Ishtar's camp.

Nine

David comes crashing into Ishtar's cave, his lungs near exploding. Ishtar and Dorinda have been eating by a small cook fire. Alarmed, Ishtar jumps to his feet and spills his plate of food in Dorinda's lap. "David! What's happened?"

David's voice barely breaks through the panting and wheezing. He leans forward, hands on knees to force out the words. "Two men - ambushed me -"

"Take a moment. Calm yourself." Ishtar leads David to the bench and urges him to sit. David takes large gulping breaths, but his words still come out spastically.

"I was following the path - Judiah cleared for me. I saw this glow - just ahead. I followed it - and it led me to a clearing. I saw the Palace across the valley -"

One final deep intake of breath and David's voice relaxes enough to speak fluently. "A volcano and all these people around performing some sort of ritual. They sacrificed one of the men to the volcano, but instead of fire, there was all this electromagnetic energy. I don't even think I could explain what actually happened."

Ishtar grimaces. "No need to. I have seen the ghastly ritual."

"Who are those people? Why are they making sacrifices? Who - *what* - are they making sacrifices to?"

Ishtar hesitates, a ruminating expression on his face. He looks questioningly to Dorinda, who is efficiently wiping the food stains from her skirt. She nods her approval.

"All of those people," Ishtar begins his story, "once inhabited this island, free and proud, with hope and promise for a bright tomorrow. But now they are slaves to the serpent ruler, the Glass Snake as we call him, because his promises have all shattered like fragile crystal."

David is thinking that this entire situation is incomprehensible. A dozen questions whirl in his head at once: *Serpent ruler? Who would worship a snake? Is he actually made of glass? What is his power over these people? How did he get it in the first place?* But he asks none of them, rendered momentarily speechless by both fascination and fear. Dorinda pours a soothing drink and offers it to David. He accepts it with trembling hands and sips it gratefully.

"Like all sacrificial rites, this one is merely a ploy to subjugate the people to stay in the Palace and do the Snake's work, too frightened to rise up and mutiny against him."

"But I didn't see any glass snake or whatever it is," David says, finding his voice again. "Just some high priestess or something."

Ishtar walks to his worktable, retrieves a small silver chest, then joins David again by the fire. From the chest, Ishtar removes a set of drawings.

"Few have actually seen the monster. With Jaycina as the Glass Snake's mediator, the people were enticed by the promise of a life of abundance instead of austerity. They worked slavishly to build a new city, with temples of learning, healing and worship, a City of Light where all could bask in the glow."

David peruses the intricate renderings that Ishtar has unfolded for him, and points to a specific spot on one of the drawings. "This is the Palace I saw. But it isn't like any ordinary castle. It's not stone. There's no turrets."

"You're right. It's far from a traditional structure. The Prism Palace is made of the finest, strongest crystal formations in the earth, skillfully sculptured and constructed. It is a wonder of architectural technology, a miracle of science and spirit combined."

"Why do you call it the Prism Palace?"

Ishtar refolds the drawings and places them back in the silver chest. "Prisms display dazzling reflections of the light spectrum," he explains knowledgeably. "They can be illuminating or deceiving." His erudite tone then shifts to intimacy. "Were you not enraptured by the heavenly aura of the Palace? Did you not want to immerse yourself in it and become one with it?"

David nods. He had felt those very things, but they had defied description.

"You saw its divinity, my boy, what it was created for. And then, at the volcano," Ishtar's tone is now angry, his face hard, "you saw its perversion, the evil that permeates the Palace under the Glass Snake's reign."

David shudders slightly and closes his eyes to blank out the memory of the sacrifice he witnessed.

"We, too, thought our lives would be transformed. Dorinda, Saliana and I. Instead we were betrayed. Jaycina used her wiles to entice us all into pledging loyalty to a new idea, an ideal, and a benevolent leader we had never seen."

"But you? Didn't you suspect - "

"Suspect it was too good to be true?" Ishtar's short laugh is an ironic one. "Yes, but my ego had the better of me. This was my opportunity to build the city of my dreams, to use all my knowledge as a scientist, my skills as an architect, and my creative vision as an artisan." Ishtar stands up and emotes theatrically, self-deprecatingly. "The rewards would be tremendous! Yes I, too, was blinded by the light of false promises. And because I was a fool, those wretched people are forced to slave in the mines, removing all the minerals, the gold, and the crystal for the perpetuation of the Glass Snake's power."

"But just what *is* his power?" David presses Ishtar for an answer, still not grasping the totality of it. "How can he control hundreds of people like this?"

Ishtar stares into the fire intently, his face reflecting the bittersweet memories of triumph and then defeat. "When the Palace was finally completed, we were all exuberant. A grand celebration was held that lasted for days. As a token of our allegiance and appreciation, we offered our personal crystals, not knowing they would be used against us."

"I don't understand what you mean by personal crystals," David says. "How can they be used against you?"

"Each of us has – or had – a gemstone given to us at birth which recorded our bio-codes, our genetic information, and all our lifetime memories. As we grew and developed, the gemstone, or personal crystal, would be imbued with all the knowledge and skill we acquired along the way. Everything we were, and would become, was recorded in the crystal. When we offered them as a token of allegiance, we had no idea that the information they contained was transferred into the Palace's Chamber of Records. When we were given our crystals back, they were completely devoid of any useful data.

"After the celebration, we all attempted to return to our homes on this side of the Island, but found they had all been destroyed. It looked as though an earthquake had hit, completely turning over the landscape.

"We were in total darkness. No light, no power, no energy and no resources in the earth to restore the light. Then we realized we had unwittingly rechanneled all of the sources of electrical energy on the Island, diverting it into the volcano and causing a seismic calamity. It is from the volcano that the Palace draws its energy source, the only source of power on the Island. With all of our sophisticated tools and equipment gone we have no means to divert it back to us for our use."

David's entire body expresses incredulity. With shrugged shoulders and pleading hands he asks the impossible, the incomprehensible. "What about the moon? The Sun? Don't tell me the Snake has turned out their lights, too?"

Ishtar nods, a solemn expression weighing heavily on his face. "In a sense he has, my son. An evil imbalance of power creates an imbalance in the universe. Until order is restored, we will not see the sun or the moon on our side of the Island."

David paces, trying to absorb it all. Head shaking, hands questioning, he debates it with himself. There are still so many unanswered questions, so many ill-fitting pieces of the puzzle. Then, bluntly, he asks Ishtar, "Why are the other people slaves and you aren't?"

Ishtar's lips are tight but trembling, his tone and his words contrite. "Because of Saliana, my daughter. She has something that the Snake covets even more than all the riches that can be mined from the earth. She has the gift of life in her song. Her beautiful voice can heal the sick, and literally bring the dying back to life. The Snake believes Saliana can make him immortal. He keeps her prisoner in the Royal Tower so she can sing for no one but him."

"And she agrees to sing for him so that her father can remain free," Dorinda says, breaking a long silence with sympathy for her friend.

"Yes. Free from the physical slavery of the mines, but never free from the slavery of guilt."

"Hush, Ishtar," Dorinda says, gently. "Feel guilty later. Now we must tell David of our plan."

David looks blankly at Dorinda. "What plan?"

Dorinda, ever the prepared one, hands David a plate of food. "Our plan to rescue Saliana," she says, a firm smile of determination lighting her friendly face.

"Dorinda, David is here to find his sister and return to his home," Ishtar says, a faint hint of hopefulness shading his words.

"Yes, Ishtar, but perhaps in rescuing Saliana he shall also rescue his Sally." Then she peers steadfastly into David's eyes. "You are at a crossroads, David, and the choice is yours," she says, finally revealing her identity.

"David stops eating, a fork held in mid-air. "It *is* you! I know it's you!" He noisily sets down the fork and plate. "You're the hologram, the Gypsy. You know where Sally is."

"Yes, I confess, I did see your Sally in my globe, but I don't know precisely where she is. Somehow she has gotten caught up in the madness of the Glass Snake's evil plans for Saliana. I don't know any more than that."

David stiffens apprehensively, and points aimlessly toward the outside of the cave. "You mean she could be there? In the Palace?"

"I feel it is possible, yes."

"Then let's go," David says, hastily moving to leave. "We've got to get her out of there."

Ishtar restrains David with a strong hand on his arm. "No, David. Wait. We cannot help. We cannot go with you."

"Why not?"

"Everyone's electro-magnetic codes, including Dorinda's and mine, were recorded in the master memory banks of the Crystal Chamber when we gave Jaycina our personal crystals. If either of us were to cross the perimeter we would immediately be detected by the security devices."

David considers this for a moment. "What about me? Could I get in? Would I be detected?"

"No, you're an unknown quantity," Ishtar says, seemingly amenable to the idea.

David is encouraged. Then, remembering his ambush, he has second thoughts. "I don't know. I don't think I could do it alone. I was almost caught by those two guards."

"Yes, that is strange," Ishtar says, obviously still irked by the incident. "You must have wandered off the path somehow."

David shakes his head emphatically. "But I didn't. I walked exactly where the path was cleared."

Ishtar expels a breath, dismissing the problem for now. "I'll speak to Judiah when I see him tomorrow. Perhaps we can devise a plan for you to enter the Palace and let us both succeed in rescuing the people that we love."

Ten

"I cannot believe you were unable to capture an unarmed boy." In her private reception room in the Prism Palace, an irate Jaycina confronts a very nervous and groveling Judiah. The brick red polished nails of her spidery hands tap impatiently on the carved ebony arms of her chair. She throws a deadly gaze at Judiah whose knees threaten to buckle under him. "Perhaps you are not worthy of your commission in my secret service."

"I beg your forgiveness, High Priestess." Judiah's hands clasped together pitifully, causing Jaycina's eyes to narrow with disdain. "The men who failed shall be properly punished. But, believe me - I, myself, could not be there to capture him. If he had seen me I would no longer be of any use to you."

"You're worthless to me now," Jaycina hisses the words.

"An unworthy wretch I am, to be sure, High Priestess. But I believe I will redeem myself when you hear of my most astounding discovery."

"It best be monumental."

"A ship, High Priestess. A magnificent sailing ship." Judiah gestures broadly and dramatically. "Sent from another world. With powers beyond your dreams, beyond anything that exists in the Prism Palace or the Glass Volcano."

Jaycina is intrigued, her posture attentive. "What kind of power?"

Seizing the moment, Judiah emotes with newfound confidence. "Crystal power. Unlimited crystal power. Three towering masts of solid crystal, surrounded by rings of pure gold."

"Where is this ship?" Jaycina's interrogation is direct now. No threatening undertones. Pointed questions requiring keen answers.

"Moored off the west shore of the Island."

"How did it get here, and when?"

"The boy, David Nickerson, sailed to the Island in that ship."

"All alone? Impossible."

"Yes, I thought so, too," Judiah speaks quickly before Jaycina's menace returns. "Until Ishtar and I read the ship's log. It is written there. He is the official captain of the ship, Moon Singer." He dares now to take a small breath of relief.

Jaycina stands in one smooth, sudden move causing Judiah to flinch and emit a small but audible gasp. But the High Priestess turns her gaze away from the weasely little man, pondering this divulgence. Finally, "Hmm. Moon Singer. A foolishly romantic name for a sailing ship."

"Begging your pardon, High Priestess, but isn't that the song Princess Saliana sings?"

"Moon Singer…yes. Yes." Jaycina pauses for reflection again. Then, sharply to Judiah, "Are you saying that Princess Saliana is singing about this ship?"

"I believe," Judiah suggests warily, "that it was her singing that called the ship here to the island."

"To escape, perhaps? With Ishtar?"

"Exactly," Judiah replies, adrenaline pumping up his words again. "The boy plans to enter the Palace undetected and rescue Saliana. We can capture him then."

Jaycina's puts her hand up as if to halt Judiah's suggestion. "No. Let him succeed. Once he is here, I will take care of him." Her eyes glow, seeming to relish the possibilities of the situation.

"As you wish," Judiah says obediently. "And the ship Moon Singer?"

"Leave it moored where it is. I will tell you when to seize it. And do not come back to the Palace or attempt to see me until I send for you."

Jaycina begins to leave the room, but Judiah brazenly scurries alongside her like a rat, pressing his limited luck dangerously further. "But how will I keep you informed, High Priestess?" he dares to protest.

Jaycina turns on her heels and glowers at him. Judiah seems to shrink into the floor. "I will find out everything I need to know, once the young Captain David Nickerson is inside the Palace. Then, be prepared for the greatest test of your allegiance to our great Serpent Ruler."

Judiah hiccups nervously, coming unstrung. "I will be prepared," he says and bows, twice, three times.

Jaycina's pomegranate lips widen in a surreptitious smile. She pivots around and, with a flourish, closes her cape around her, exiting regally.

Eleven

Retracing David's steps, Ishtar and Judiah inspect the path where David had been accosted the previous day.

"You see, Ishtar, this is the path I cleared. It's nowhere near the Palace boundary. The boy must have wandered off his course."

"Yes, possibly," Ishtar says, considering Judiah's conclusion. "But he swears he followed your directions. Could there be an opening you didn't see? Perhaps an animal tore away the brush."

"Possibly - possibly." Judiah's tone suggests they not consider this possibility at all.

"Or," Ishtar says, creating another scenario, "the guards knew that David would be walking alone and deliberately led him into a trap by diverting the path."

"But how could they know, Ishtar? We were the only ones…Oh, no, surely you don't suspect that I… Ishtar, we are friends too long. I am insulted."

Judiah's exaggerated indignation and pouty face are almost comical, leading Ishtar to wave his hand in dismissal. "Calm yourself, Judiah. I am not accusing you. I'm merely trying to solve this puzzle."

"Of course, of course," Judiah responds with a slightly giddy laugh. "I know you are under great strain because of Saliana." He pauses a moment, then couches his words. "You know, Ishtar, what do we really know of this David Nickerson? How do we know he can be trusted?"

Now Ishtar is irritated. "What are you implying?"

"Perhaps he was not ambushed at all. Perhaps he lied."

"And why would the boy lie?"

"To throw us off, to keep us from discovering his real reason for coming to the Island."

Ishtar looks at Judiah squarely, his tone blunt. "And just what would that be?"

"To take Saliana away with him - away from you - forever."

Twelve

Later, David helps Ishtar light a series of candles in his cave to cast extra light on his worktable. Ishtar arranges his tools carefully on the table then spreads out a bolt of white cloth that has the texture and suppleness of doeskin. Ishtar holds out his hand. "Give me your pouch of crystals, David." David does.

Ishtar spreads the stones out on top of the fabric and examines each one of them with a gem cutter's eye glass.

"Do you really think this will work?" David asks.

"It will, if the gridwork pattern is properly constructed."

"If you recall," David says, his tone ironic, "it was a gridwork pattern that got me into this predicament."

"But this time," the older man replies with a wise twinkle, "you will be wearing it." As they converse, Ishtar cuts a section of the cloth into a tunic and begins fitting it to David's body, making tailor's marks in strategic places with a piece of colored chalk.

"The stones will be sewn into this garment, one on each apex of the four triangles."

"Four triangles? Holy cow. That means twelve points – a *double* Star of David."

"Twice as powerful," Ishtar says, pointing the chalk at David with emphasis, "as the gridwork pattern that transported you here."

"Holy cow. I could wind up on the moon. Or Venus!"

Ishtar laughs jovially. "A mere stone's throw away from your United States. You are already farther into the Universe's dimensions than that."

David's face registers shock, surprise, then elation. "Farther than Venus? What do you mean? Where am I?"

Ishtar uses a delicate touch to chisel and cut each crystal to the desired size and shape. He pauses now and then, not speaking so that he can concentrate on the exacting task. One slip and the crystal would crumble into powder.

"Where do you think you are?"

David shrugs and exhales a hard breath, as if to say he hasn't the faintest idea. "Frankly, I think this whole thing is a dream. Or maybe I'm out of my mind."

"Ah. Perfect cut," Ishtar says, complimenting his own handiwork. He then sets the chiseled crystal aside and picks up another one. "Whether it's a dream," he says after a moment, "or an illusion, or all in your mind, doesn't matter. They are all merely different levels of the same consciousness."

"Please. No more riddles." David makes a weary plea. "Tell me the truth, Ishtar. Where am I?"

Ishtar lays down his tools and gazes piercingly into David's eyes. The look seems to consider whether or not David is ready to hear the truth, or even comprehend it. He ventures forth.

"The Star of David gridwork is a sacred geometric form. Each point in the star represents the ideals to which man aspires on their highest level. The top three points," Ishtar explains as he touches each apex, "are Mercy and Justice with Power at the center apex. The bottom three are Love and Wisdom with Truth at the center point. Triangle upon triangle, laid in opposite directions, weaves these principles into a tapestry of interactive forces. Had you known what you were doing when you invoked its power, you would now exist in a state of dynamic equilibrium between your earthly self and your higher self."

"Dynamic what?" David is truly nonplussed, his expression vacant.

"A state of total enlightenment, my boy, where knowledge is infinite and mysteries are solved in a miniscule particle of time." Ishtar's face illuminates at the wonder of it all. Then, it registers surrender to the circumstances. "But, since you are here by accident and not by design -"

"I'm in some sort of etheric limbo."

"We call it the hole in reality."

"You mean like a black hole?"

"No." Ishtar resumes cutting and polishing the crystals. "A black hole is a phenomenon of astronomical space, measurable by physical science. A hole in reality is a psychic phenomenon, measurable only by your own metaphysical awareness."

Ishtar adjusts the fit of the tunic on David's shoulders and ties off a basting stitch, then motions for David to remove the garment.

David shakes his head and scratches it, completely bewildered. "This is all too confusing for me." Then, the enormity of the situation clicks in and David nods, his emotions deflating. "I screwed up, didn't I?"

Ishtar begins to draw the gridwork pattern on the tunic, marking where each of the twelve crystals is to be sewn. "In prosaic terms, yes."

"Great. Now what?"

"Now," Ishtar says with bold encouragement, "we correct the 'screw up' and reverse the dynamics of the situation. That's why I doubled the gridwork pattern."

As David watches Ishtar work deftly and intently, an unexpected feeling of affection and admiration for this man fills his heart. Ishtar is so much like his father, with that same unyielding dedication to his craft, the same meticulous attention to the smallest detail.

"You know, it's funny," David ruminates aloud, "how your problems are so similar, yours and my dad's. He feels like it's his fault Sally can't walk, and you feel guilty about Saliana being up in that tower. All because your work meant more to both of you than anything else. If I didn't know better, I'd swear you were the same person, or brothers at least."

"We are all interconnected, David. Kindred souls who touch time and time again under different circumstances, for different reasons."

"And sometimes by accident," David says glumly, referring to himself. "Ishtar - did I - did my botched experiment with the grid patterns cause your problems? The Snake, Saliana being captive, and all that?"

Ishtar places a fatherly hand on David's shoulder. "No, no, my boy. We merely had an inter-dimensional collision. It happens often, causing destinies to become intertwined in unexplainable ways. Perhaps it is really our good fortune, and not our dilemma."

David moves his own hand up to touch Ishtar's in a mutual gesture of kinship. Their eyes meet and, in that moment of time, the bond between them is fixed throughout eternity.

In a few hours the gridwork pattern is finished, except for one final and crucial crystal. Ishtar picks up a stone that looks like broken charcoal and holds it up to the candlelight. It is translucent in spite of its dark color.

"This is a piece of Moldavite," Ishtar informs David, "the last one of its kind on the Island." As he sews it into the tunic with a gold thread, his admonition is foreboding. "You must not lose the Moldavite, especially if you encounter the High Priestess Jaycina. It is your only means of communication with me and Dorinda."

"Communication? How?"

"David, how did you lose your hearing?"

"I had otosclerosis when I was seven. The doctors operated several times, but my left ear never responded. My right ear can hear only very loud noises or speech, even with my hearing aid."

"Seven years old. This is why you still speak so well," Ishtar concludes. "There's barely any indication of a speech impediment. Tell me, is your hearing loss sensorineural or conductive?"

"Both, but mostly sensorineural. The sounds get into my inner ear, but my brain can't quite interpret them."

"But here, you can hear normally. This is good. It means you are vibrationally attuned to the Island's frequency, and it means that the Moldavite will work quite well. You know, of course, that crystals are used to control radio frequencies in electronic equipment."

"Yes. In fact, I have an old crystal set my grandfather left me. It still works," David says casually. Then it occurs to him, "But - how do you know about electronic equipment?"

"Never mind that now," Ishtar says brusquely, indicating this is not the time to change the subject. "The Moldavite's power to transmit and amplify sound is superior. This means that you will be able to hear me speak to you, word for word, through your hearing instrument which will be picking up the Moldavite's sound vibrations.

"But if you lose contact with us," Ishtar forewarns David, "you will be completely at Jaycina's mercy, and she has none. She will try to beguile you, seduce you with her beauty. If this fails, she will bewitch you, and your eyes will be unable to see what your heart knows is true."

Ishtar ties off the sewing thread and helps David put on the tunic. His costume is now complete, having already relinquished the white deck pants, blue jersey and sneakers that were ruined in his fall. Now David wears the suede boots and snug pants that Dorinda tailored for him and, topped by the crystal-laden tunic, he feels an inner power he has never experienced. But then an obvious, disturbing thought occurs to him.

"But what if Jaycina sees the crystals - the gridwork?"

Ishtar holds up another garment, emerald green in color made of a sturdy woven fabric. "You will wear this vest over it to conceal it." Ishtar places his hand over David's heart. "As long as Jaycina does not touch you here, the Moldavite will stay intact."

David slips on the vest and laces up the front. Next, Ishtar shows David a ring with a large, clear, pyramid-cut stone. It shall be his ultimate weapon against Jaycina's inscrutable powers.

"Jaycina wears a white diamond ring that looks like this," Ishtar briefs David. "If you are detected and caught, you must somehow find a way to remove her diamond ring and replace it with this one. When it has worked its magic, it will turn blue and you will know her heart has found Truth - the one force Jaycina is powerless against."

Ishtar gives David the pyramid ring, which he recommends stay hidden in the cuff of David's boot. Then he hands David the most precious gem of all. "Don't forget this. Your Singer."

David holds the treasured crystal in his hand for a moment, wistfully recalling the first moment he saw it. How he wishes he was back home in his own living room when any thoughts of mystical adventures were merely fantasies. He places the Singer in the tunic's pocket.

When Judiah enters Ishtar's cave, Ishtar's eyes narrow suspiciously, but he does not give voice to the doubts that have been plaguing him. After all, he did ask Judiah to report to him regarding David's accessibility to the Prism Palace. He has no choice but to risk the mission to rescue Saliana on Judiah's professed loyalty.

"I have timed the sequence of the patrol," Judiah announces to Ishtar, with a slight inflection of self-importance. "When the rituals are taking place, the guards do not patrol the path. They guard the temple."

"Good. This will enable David to cross the perimeter undetected."

"Yes, Ishtar. There are fewer men available to check the grounds." Then, to David, "When one sentry goes by, that will be your chance to scale the Palace wall." His tone softens to shades of feigned comradeship. "Good luck, lad. I will be close by at all times to help if you should need me. But you won't be able to see me. Just know that I am there."

Thirteen

David makes his way carefully along the path to the Palace grounds, then halts just outside the forbidden zone and conceals himself in the brush. A sentry walks by on his patrol, then disappears from view. Knowing this is his chance, David sprints across the grounds to the Palace courtyard. Unlike the view of the Palace he first glimpsed from across the meadow, one of spectacular radiance, this side of the Palace is dim and shadowy, like the dark side of the moon.

Hovering low to the ground, David creeps along the west exterior trying to get as close to the Tower as possible before attempting to enter. At last, he sees the Tower straight above his head. But how in the world can he get up there?

He feels around for some grooves in the surface to grab on to so he can scale the walls. But the facade is slick and smooth and impossible to climb.

"Oh, great. This is like climbing a wall of ice," he grumbles. Why can't it be like a real medieval castle, he thinks, with some ridges to dig his boots into? Then, something along the side of the wall catches David's eye and he walks toward it.

"Oh, no way. A rope? This is almost too good to be true."

He looks around warily. The landscape around him is still and dead quiet. Not a sound, not a sense of anything moving nearby.

Too good or not, David grabs onto the rope and jumps up, letting it take his full weight. He jumps back to the ground.

It just might work, he decides.

Once again, David grabs onto the rope and pulls himself up onto it. Inch by inch, he painstakingly climbs its full length toward the window of the Tower.

From an obscure nearby place, Judiah and a sentry stand together watching David scale the Tower wall using the conveniently-placed rope.

"Good work," Judiah commends the sentry. "The boy is in. Jaycina will take over from here. Be certain you're not detected by anyone when you cut down the rope."

Accepting the few pieces of gold Judiah offers him, the sentry nods stoically then rushes off.

Exhausted from the climb, David glances down at the ground below and tries to steady himself on the window ledge. A sudden wave of vertigo sets his head spinning. His lunch threatens to regurgitate. He leans his head against the portal and, remembering a little trick his mother taught him, David presses his palms together in a prayer-like gesture. He stares intently at the vertical line of his hands. In a moment his dizziness subsides.

Exhaling deeply, relieved, David steps off the window ledge and into the Tower. Remembering the Moldavite, he places his hand over his heart and speaks in a forced whisper. "Ishtar. Ishtar, if you can hear me, I'm inside the Palace up in the Tower."

In his cave dwelling, Ishtar's nervous waiting for David's voice is over. He holds a large quartz crystal, which is curved and hollowed like a conch shell, up to his ear.

Elation fills his voice. "He made it! He's in the Palace Tower." Dorinda huddles close to Ishtar's crystal earphone trying to hear for herself.

David strains to hear something, anything, in return from Ishtar. Then, faintly, it comes through. "I am receiving you, David. Can you hear me, my boy?"

"Holy cow!" David is amazed to hear Ishtar's voice through his hearing aid. "Yes, I can hear you."

"Good. Wonderful. Now, carefully, go and look for Saliana."

Stealthily, David moves further ahead into gleaming hallways of the Tower, each surface as slick as the Palace wall. Were it not for his sturdy boots, he surmises, he surely would go slipping and sliding across the floor as though it were an ice arena.

Then, he hears it, something oddly familiar. But he cannot connect it to any recollection. A few more steps and the sweet sounds of Saliana playing the harp and singing fill the air:

"I know a place where the Moon Dancers waltz

In gossamer gowns and slippers of stardust.

On velvety royal blue carpets of nighttime

They step light as air to the music of wind songs..."

He tiptoes into the room behind Saliana. She does not hear him and continues singing:

"Moon Singer, Moon Singer, take to the sea,

Fly on the wind where the sky used to be.

Moon Singer, Moon Singer, take me along.

Keep me safe in your light till I find my way home."

Entranced with her singing, David clumsily trips on something underfoot. Startled, Saliana turns to see him. Her breath catches in her throat.

"Who are you? How did you get in here?"

David stares at her, blankly, captivated by her fragile loveliness. If he had not heard her angelic singing for himself, he would never have believed that this delicate girl's music held such divine powers.

"That's the most beautiful song I've ever heard," David tells her, still not connecting her music to the song he heard the day Sally disappeared. Recognizing the questioning look in her large brown eyes, he announces, "Your father sent me."

At once alarmed and elated, Saliana moves toward David. "My father sent you? Is he - is he all right? Nothing's happened?"

"No, no. He's fine," David assures her. He wonders why he can't stop staring at her. Then he notices the rose crystal pendant she wears around her neck, and it hits him.

"You look so much like Sally. Just like Sally."

Fourteen

Saliana's puzzled expression asks, "Who is Sally?" But she voices a more personally pressing question. "Did you come to take me home?" David reawakens to the mission at hand, which is rescuing the frightened young damsel in distress who stands before him.

"Your father seems to think I can. I'm not sure how."

"It will be impossible." All hope seems drained from her, perhaps long ago. "Even Father could not rescue me from *him*."

Remembering her song lyrics, David shifts the subject again. "How do you know about the Moon Singer?"

A thoughtful expression crosses Saliana's face. She considers this question a moment. "I don't know, really. I began singing the song when I was first imprisoned here. It just came to me one night. I feel it has a special meaning, so I continue to sing it. Do you know the song?"

"No. I don't know. There's something familiar about it. But I know the Moon Singer itself. That's the name of the clipper ship that brought me here."

"You sailed here?" She is at once bemused and contemptuous. "Why would you want to come to our island? It's such a terrible place." Her tone then becomes wistful.

"But it wasn't always. Once there was a lot of music and singing. Everyone was so happy, so alive. But now…"

"Who is Sally?" she asks, focusing back on David's earlier comment.

"It's a long story. I'll tell you after I get you out of here."

"But how?"

"The same way I came in. The rope hanging down the Tower wall. Come on, quick."

David takes Saliana's hand and leads her out of her chamber to the hallway, then to the window he entered from. He steps out onto the ledge, ready to assist her over and down to freedom, but he stops short.

"Holy cow - wait!" David pulls up the rope and it's only a few feet long. It's been cleanly cut. "I thought it was too good to be true."

"So did I."

"There must be some other way out," David surmises, hoping there truly is, "or your Father would never have sent me here."

Suddenly, the monstrous roar is heard and a thunderous thud and rattle looms close to Saliana's chamber.

"Holy cow! What's that?" Fear pulses through David's body and he blanches white, then flushes red with an adrenaline rush.

"The Glass Snake! He's coming. Quickly. You must hide!"

David scans the hall quickly and sees no hiding place. "Hide where?"

"We must go back to my chamber," Saliana urges him. "If I'm gone he'll suspect something." As they rush to Saliana's chamber, the roar of the Snake is deafening.

"Oh, my God. He's right next door. Here! Under the portal." Saliana nudges David toward the wall and pushes on his shoulders till he slides to the floor. "Stay tight to the wall. He won't be able to see you there."

Quickly, Saliana snatches up her harp, sits on her chair and begins to sing, her voice quivering with terror. The Snake's blood red eyes peer through the portal at her, and it bellows with pleasure at the sound of her music. David anchors himself firmly against the wall, afraid to even imagine what this *Thing* looks like.

After what seems an eternity, the Snake calms down, then thuds and rumbles away. David exhales loudly with relief. Sweat trickles down his brow. He tries to stand up, but his legs are jelly.

"He'll be gone for awhile," Saliana says, helping David to his feet. "The rituals are going on in the temple and they last for hours."

Blood starts to circulate back in David's legs and he shakes them back to full strength. "Good. That'll give me time to scout around for a way out of the Palace."

"Be careful of Jaycina," Saliana warns him, not unlike her father. "Don't let her catch you."

"Your father warned me, too. But he gave me some special crystals to protect me."

"Please, please come back," she pleads. "I so want to go home."

"So do I, Saliana. So do I."

Fifteen

Exploring deeper into the Palace, David finds himself engulfed in a labyrinth of mirrored corridors. He turns this way and that, unable to find an opening or a way out. The complex maze, the hundreds of multi-colored illusory images, confuse his brain and the vertigo begins again. David struggles to keep his balance and swallows hard on the bile that works its way up his throat.

Focus, he tells himself. *Focus on the floor, on the seams along the floor where it meets the walls.* But there aren't any discernible walls. Just row after row of his own distorted reflection bouncing back at him. He places his hand over the Moldavite.

"Ishtar. Ishtar, are you there? I can't find my way through these corridors."

"David!" Ishtar responds sharply. "Where in the world have you been? Why haven't you contacted me? And how in the world did you get caught in the maze?"

"Well, when I left the Tower, I turned to the left - Oh, great." Filled with recrimination for not communicating with Ishtar, he chastises himself. "How could I forget? I saw Saliana. She's fine, or at least as fine as she can be."

"Thank heaven! Thank heaven." Ishtar's voice is a litany of emotions: relief, gratitude, guilt, then determination, authority. "You must get her out of there, David. Listen carefully. If you are in the maze of mirrors you are in the East wing of the Palace near the Temple. Follow the blue mirrors until you come to the hidden staircase. I will direct you from there."

David squints hard to locate the blue mirrors among the kaleidoscopic shimmer of all the others. Finally, he isolates them. "There they are, Ishtar. I see them."

David follows their pattern with his hands, feeling for an opening where the staircase might be located. A strange, muffled throbbing sound catches his attention and he stops for a moment to listen. He can't quite discern what the sound is, but it is rhythmical and pulsating. It becomes louder, more intriguing, and beckons to him. David slips behind one of the mirrors and into the shadows just as another message comes from Ishtar, strangely premonitory.

"David, if you should hear the sounds of chanting, do not let them entice you. Stay away from the Temple."

"Too late. I think I'm there."

In a loft above the Altar of Initiation, David views the Temple interior below him. Jaycina is once again officiating over some bizarre ceremony. Seeing her this closely, David can feel her captivating power. *No wonder Ishtar was bedazzled by her.* The temple, with its sleek white walls and modernistic architecture, are a confusing contrast to the Gothic ambience of Ishtar's cave and the eccentric clothes he and Dorinda wear. Even more contradictory is the crystal chamber's futuristic holographic console, juxtaposed with the primitive beliefs that such a ritual represents.

Jaycina gestures dramatically with her crystal scepter, then turns to the image of the Serpent Ruler high above the Altar. Hundreds of subjects kneel on the crystalline steps and, at Jaycina's prompting, they chant their mantra, "Hail! Hail! Ruler of All. King of all. Hail!" The Temple musicians play a spirited tribute, while the Temple dancers whirl about the Altar and lay flowers and gifts beneath the Serpent's image.

"Holy cow," David says, audibly. But the din drowns out his remark. "This is unreal. They'll never believe me back home."

"David! David, get out of there, now!" Ishtar's command bellows in David's ear and he is shaken out of his enraptured state. Reluctantly, he leaves the loft and returns to the Palace corridor.

"Ishtar," David calls softly. "I'm just outside the Temple. I have to look around some more. I want to know what's going on. I have to know if Sally's here."

"I must warn you against it," Ishtar says forcefully. "It's too dangerous. The longer you are there the more distorted your perception will become. Once you know the way to freedom, you must go back for Saliana and get out as fast as you can."

But David is a brother determined to find his sister. "I'll be careful, I promise." He presses his hand on the Moldavite as though to secure it even more snugly in place in his tunic. "As long as I can keep in touch with you, I'll be fine."

Further on, David comes to a chamber door. Feeling adventuresome, he enters, not as cautious as he should be at this juncture. The chamber is a mini-maze of illusion, with mirrored panels of every color reflecting everything in the room dozens of times, including David himself. He looks around the chamber, squinting out the prismatic glare, and discovers what appears to be the door to a closet. Feeling for an edge, and finding it, David opens the door. The closet is filled with ceremonial gowns, jewels and headdresses eerily set on mannequin forms, which look like faceless Jaycinas.

"This must be Jaycina's chamber. What luck."

He closes the closet door. Startled to see the reflection of someone beside him, he spins on his heels and faces Jaycina square on.

"What luck, indeed," she says, wearing her Cheshire cat grin.

David's stomach churns wildly. Fear burns a hole in his chest. But he attempts to be cavalier.

"Uh - oh - Hi, there. Guess I'm in the wrong room. Well, I'll be leaving now."

"So soon?" Jaycina slinks toward him. David shrinks back. "Why, you've just arrived. Please stay and let me demonstrate my hospitality."

David clears his throat, but the words squeak out in an adolescent tenor. "Uh - yeah. Well, that's a very tempting offer, but I'm late for an appointment."

"What could be more important than being here with me? I promise you it will be an experience you will long remember."

"I'll bet," David remarks under his breath.

"David! Get out. Now." Ishtar's alarmed plea bellows in David's ear. David's hand goes up instinctively to shroud the sound.

Jaycina circles David slowly, as though examining him from head to toe. The room begins to move in quivering waves. David begins to see double and he shakes his head to refocus. Jaycina dissolves into a prismatic light, then reverts back to human form. This transformation occurs several times until David stumbles, stupefied, about the room. Dizzy from the combination of Ishtar's frantic orders in his hearing aid and Jaycina's mesmerizing tricks, David flops down on Jaycina's chaise lounge, unable to stand up any longer.

She seats herself so close to him that her breath tickles his face. Her kohl black eyes and gilded lids are garish but strangely attractive, David thinks, and he can hardly believe he thinks so.

"What a handsome vest," Jaycina croons. "But it must be very warm. Why not take it off for awhile and be comfortable." She toys with the laces that keep the vest closed to hide the magic tunic beneath.

David draws back to avoid her touch. "No! I mean, I'm fine. Cold, in fact."

"Such a sweet boy. So handsome, so innocent." With one swift tug, Jaycina unlaces David's vest to reveal the tunic. The crystals glitter, their reflections dancing in the light of the mirrored room.

"Exquisite," Jaycina comments, in a Marilyn Monroe sort of breathiness. "The most beautiful tunic I have ever seen."

"Oh, this old thing? You should see my Sunday tunic." David makes a feeble attempt at humor, at the same time wiping beads of sweat that bubble up on his forehead.

"Such an unusual design." Jaycina reaches over and runs her hand along the Star of David gridwork pattern. David quickly places his hand over his heart to protect the Moldavite stone. But Jaycina is too cunning. With a rapid flick of her talon-like fingernails, she cuts David's hand, drawing blood. Instinctively, he puts his hand up to his mouth and sucks on it to stop the blood. In a deft move, Jaycina plucks the Moldavite from its hiding place.

"What a lovely gift," Jaycina says coyly, her eyes relishing the rare and valuable black stone. "Thank you, David. I've always wanted one."

"Don't mention it."

When Jaycina rises from the chaise lounge, David blows out a big breath of defeat and murmurs, "Damn. I've just been disconnected."

Sixteen

Huddling behind a rock formation on the beach, a distressed Ishtar and Dorinda watch as a crew of men rowing several large boats tow the Moon Singer away from what they thought was a secure hiding place.

Anger, confusion, and disbelief flush Ishtar's face. "I can't understand it. How did they discover the Moon Singer?"

Dorinda's anger matches Ishtar's, but she is far more certain of the reason. "There is no other explanation, Ishtar. David was detected entering the Palace. This enabled Jaycina to ensnare him."

"But how? She has no crystal imprint on David to detect him. And Judiah had the guard's schedule timed perfectly."

Dorinda's mouth is tight, her eyes hard as steel. "Perhaps Judiah had more than the guard's schedule timed perfectly."

"What do you mean?"

"Look closely." Dorinda motions toward a group of men now congregating on the shore, and one in particular whose face is lighted by the lantern he carries.

Ishtar's body becomes rigid, his voice leaden with contempt. "Judiah. Judiah, the traitor." He moves to confront the man he once called his friend.

"No." Dorinda restrains him with a firm hand. "Wait. He mustn't know we've discovered him. Not yet. Our time will come to expose him for the turncoat that he is. First, we must know where they will hide the Moon Singer."

Ishtar clenches his hand into a fist, and presses it hard against his mouth, as though to hold back a tirade of acrimony from escaping his lips. Silently, he nods in agreement and he and Dorinda move quietly in the shadows to follow the men.

* * *

David sits awkwardly on plush satin pillows while Jaycina reclines next to him. Slave girls fan them with large peacock feathers and serve them food and wine. Jaycina toys with David, kittenishly, plopping grapes in his mouth and giving him sips of wine from a gold chalice.

This is like a scene out of a bad movie, David thinks. He has been playing the bumpkin, the ignoramus, hoping that Jaycina will believe he is not worth detaining. Certainly not capable of outsmarting her and rescuing Saliana.

"So, Jaycina. You're a high priestess. That must be a very important job. Don't you have to go to the Altar or something now?"

"How quaint you are." Jaycina's merry laugh is nonetheless chilling. "No. There will be no more rituals tonight. I have found something more interesting to amuse me."

"Uh - yeah, well, what about this Serpent Ruler. The Glass Snake or whatever. Isn't he going to need you for something?"

One of the slave girls takes Jaycina's outstretched hand and helps her rise to her feet. "The Great Serpent Ruler needs me for everything." Her onyx eyes narrow to slits as she speaks softly, but menacingly. "Without me, he would crumble to ashes and die."

"Not as long as he has Saliana," David ventures a stab at her. "Not as long as she sings for him."

The High Priestess sits patiently in her imperial chair while a slave girl adjusts her gown carefully around her feet. She is kittenish again, almost indifferent in her expression. "Oh, yes. The little child in the Tower." She smirks cynically. "He thinks she has the power of immortality in her song."

Relieved to be free of Jaycina's cloying advances, David rises to his feet. "Doesn't she?"

Jaycina studies David a moment, considering her response, which is then cryptic. "Only if he thinks she does."

David's reaction is a blank stare, revealing nothing of what he truly feels. "Are you telling me that Saliana's music has no power? Then why is she being held captive and made to sing for him?"

"Oh, her music has power, no doubt. But immortality comes from a far greater source than Saliana's little song."

"You mean God?"

Jaycina dismisses "God" with an arrogant sniff. "God. The term is an abstraction. The power, the force that gives and sustains life is real. It exists. And whoever finds it and claims it for his - for *her* - own, will be the immortal one."

"How can you find it? If it isn't in Saliana's song, then where is it? What is it?"

"Of that, my sly boy, I'm not sure. So, for now, Saliana must sing. Perhaps somewhere in her song is a clue." She scrutinizes David's face for any sign that she has

touched a nerve. His face remains impassive. "Besides," she adds offhandedly, "it pleases the Glass Snake to hear her."

"You mean you're deceiving him until you figure out the power thing for yourself?"

Jaycina's nostrils flare slightly at the insinuation, but once again she manipulates the conversation her way and baits David. "Given the chance, isn't everyone capable of deceiving others? Haven't you been deceived by Ishtar and Dorinda about why you are here, in the Palace?"

Finally, David's body responds, stiffening with apprehension. "What do you mean? Why would they deceive me?"

Jaycina purses her lips, registering pleasure that she has at last pricked his emotional armor. "So that you will rescue Saliana, thinking that in doing so you will find your sister."

David is unnerved. *How could she know about Sally?* His non-chalant facade begins to crack. "What do you know about my sister?"

"All I need to know." Jaycina rises to stand close to him. "She is the most important person in your life, so important that you sailed that immense clipper ship all alone to this island. That was very brave of you, David, very brave and unselfish." She runs a fuchsia-colored fingernail seductively along his cheek. David's skin quivers, but he stands still as a stone. "I could use someone like you in the Palace. You are brave and you are loyal, among other things. Together we could control the infinite power of the Glass Volcano, rule the City, share the wealth. Perhaps even have your Sally here with you."

Now, David's eyes glow hot and threatening. He jerks his body slightly, clenches his fists. "Wait a minute. Do you know where Sally is? Do you? If you do, you'd better tell me or - "

"No, I don't know where your Sally is," Jaycina says with a cool, unaffected calm. "But possibly I could help you find her."

"How." David is insistent.

"I cannot divulge any secrets," she says evasively, "unless of course I felt you were worthy of my trust."

"And what would convince you?"

"Come with me to the tunnels," she invites him, "and we will see."

Through a secret passageway from her chamber, David follows Jaycina to the mines. They are a stark contrast from the glistening interior Palace halls above ground. Here in the mine tunnels, hundreds of men labor relentlessly in the eerie yellow light, gleaning crystals and gemstones from the rocky walls.

Sweat glistens on their bodies as they strain from the grueling work and the unbearable heat. If they falter, they are whipped. They beg for water, but are denied more than a swallow.

It is incredible, David thinks, that people can treat other people this way in this day and age. But then, what day and age is this? Past? Present? Future? *Where in God's name am I? And how in hell do I get out?*

"It's like an oven in here! How can these men stand it? What gives you the right to treat them like this?"

"It is the life they have chosen as part of their allegiance to the Serpent Ruler."

David finds Jaycina's statement ironic. "I don't think this is what they had in mind as part of the deal."

"We all must live with the choices we make, David," she says maternally.

"If we have a choice, you mean."

"Everyone has a choice, including you, dear boy. You can choose to stay, or you can choose to go. I will not stop you."

He faces Jaycina square on, casts her a wary eye. "You mean you would let me leave here? Take Saliana, too?"

"Of course I would," Jaycina says, amenably. "But there is a condition attached."

"Which is?"

"If you choose to give up your quest to find Sally, you may go any time."

David scoffs at this ridiculous stipulation, and ignores her reference to Sally as preposterous. What is she really up to? "Why did you bring me down here? It's not winning you any points."

Jaycina waxes pious, almost comically. "So you may see for yourself the wonders of the Prism Palace, and tell everyone of the work done here for the glory of our great Serpent Ruler."

David finds her proselytizing repulsive. "If you mean tell people how you keep these men in slavery, killing them in these tunnels, you bet I would. I couldn't let you get away with this."

"But you are wrong, David. These men are quite happy. Look a little closer. Tell me what your eyes see."

As though her hand is a sorcerer's wand, Jaycina gestures rapidly and broadly. A spiral of light suddenly funnels across the mind shaft, swift as a cyclone. A magnificent rainbow of colors flashes wildly, changing the very ambiance of the dreary underground. Finally, an aura of peace and tranquility settles in the tunnel.

Instead of the horrible cruelty that he witnessed only seconds before, David now sees a colony of men working contentedly, singing as they work, laughing and making light conversation as they eat and drink. David rubs his eyes, shakes his head, in disbelief.

"This is not happening. It's some sort of magic trick."

"The only trick is in your mind, David. What your eyes see is what is true."

"*Beware,*" David remembers Ishtar's prophetic warning, "*... your eyes will be unable to see what your heart knows is true.*"

Seventeen

Nothing would have given Ishtar more pleasure than to have Dorinda sprinkle some rat poison in the delectable, simmering stew, then watch as the rodent Judiah choked and gasped his agonizing final breath. No one but Dorinda could have talked him out of such a notion, for Ishtar trusted her ingenuity in seeing that Judiah got his just desserts.

Now, as Dorinda and Ishtar play host to the traitor in their midst, Judiah gorges himself in blissful ignorance of their desire for vengeance.

"This is wonderful, wonderful, Dorinda. I've always said you were the best cook on the Island," Judiah gushes. He holds out his plate and Dorinda serves him another huge helping of stew.

"Right now, she's the *only* cook on the Island," Ishtar quips. His friendly smile is an odd contrast to his eyes which are laser beams of rage.

Judiah laughs heartily, never taking his own eyes off the sumptuous fare, the kind of food he hasn't had in months. "Always one with a sense of humor, Ishtar."

"It seems to run in my family," Ishtar says, and pours more wine into Judiah's generous-sized goblet.

"Why else would a man be given a woman's name?" Dorinda plays along.

"Yes, it's true. Mother had quite a sense of humor. Father was not so amused."

"Ah, but your namesake is legendary, just as you will be one day," Judiah says, lavishing praise on Ishtar in his usual bootlicking manner. "You were meant for greatness, my friend. It is your destiny."

Ishtar's mood turns serious. "My destiny will not be fulfilled, I fear, not as long as Saliana is imprisoned." He shifts to restrained eagerness. "So, tell me, what news have you of David?"

Judiah casts a sidelong glance at Ishtar, as though afraid to meet the man's eyes straight on. Eating is a convenient protective device. "I have heard nothing since he scaled the Tower wall."

"Nor has he communicated with me through the Moldavite," Ishtar says, voicing sincere concern.

Judiah stops eating, but his mouth is full. Now, he dares to look at Ishtar, his expression a mixture of apprehension and opportunity. "You fear he is captured?"

Ishtar nods. "I can think of no other reason he hasn't contacted me. Can you?"

Judiah hesitates. He swallows the stew loudly. "I hesitate to say, Ishtar," he begins prudently, then seizes the opportunity. "But you know that I am not quite certain of the boy's motives."

"If you did not trust him, Judiah, why did you help him get inside the Palace grounds?" Ishtar treads lightly, but emphatically.

"Why, for you, Ishtar." Judiah's response is a fusion of feigned indignation and ardor. "How could I deny you your hope that Saliana would be rescued? If I were wrong about the boy, I could never forgive myself for not helping."

Ishtar pats Judiah's shoulder fraternally. "Always there when I need you." He and Dorinda lock eyes, knowingly. "Yes, you are a good friend. Here. A bit more wine." Ishtar lifts the carafe to pour but, suddenly, he grabs his chest in pain, spilling the wine all over Judiah.

"Ishtar! What is it?" Judiah's brows form shaggy parentheses around his shocked eyes.

Ishtar groans, staggers about the cave, falls over his work table, then slumps to the floor. Dorinda and Judiah rush to his side.

Dorinda cries hysterically. "Ishtar! Ishtar. Speak to me. Please!"

"My God," Judiah gasps. "Is he - dead?"

Ishtar stirs slightly, flutters his eyes, and tries to speak, but only manages a forced whisper. "Judiah - come closer."

Judiah bends a little closer and Ishtar pulls him down by his shirtfront, bringing them both nose to nose.

"Get word to David - and Saliana. Tell her - I love her - tell her she can stop singing now -" He closes his eyes, breathes a labored last breath, and falls limp.

Dorinda is grief stricken. "Ishtar! No! Oh, no."

"Is he dead *now*?"

Dorinda cradles her dear friend in her arms. "Yes. He is dead."

Eighteen

Dorinda wipes her eyes with her scarf and blows her nose into it. "Oh, it was all too much for him. Poor, tormented, Ishtar," she wails dramatically. "Now he'll never know if Saliana is rescued.

"What did he mean - tell Saliana she can stop singing now?" Judiah's voice trembles, like someone who knows he is in trouble but not quite sure how deep.

"Well," Dorinda says, regaining her composure, "you know that Saliana only agreed to sing for the Glass Snake to assure that Ishtar would be safe." Judiah nods. "But now that he's –" She begins to wail again. Judiah pats her shoulder gingerly. Clearing her throat and restraining her emotions, Dorinda continues. "As soon as Saliana stops singing, the Snake will begin to weaken. He will no longer be invincible."

Judiah's mouth pops open in stunned silence. "You mean he could possibly be slain by someone?" Judiah shudders as though surprised that such a suggestion could come from his own mouth.

"Oh, yes," Dorinda says matter-of-factly. "And very easily, too."

Judiah dares to ask, "How?"

"Cut off his tail and he will die." Dorinda graphically illustrates this with a deft swipe at the air with an imaginary knife. Judiah jerks back from her motion.

"His tail?" Judiah is totally baffled, but attempts to conceal his ignorance. "Yes, yes, of course. His tail."

"Go, now, Judiah," Dorinda requests sadly. "I must prepare my friend for his voyage to eternity."

"Can I help you bury him?" Judiah's tone seems slightly eager, then shifting oddly to commiseration, he adds quickly, "My poor friend, Ishtar."

"Come back in an hour and you can help me carry him to the beach where the Moon Singer is moored. That's a good spot."

"The beach? But - no, no you can't bury him in the sand with all those crabs and scavenger birds," Judiah protests. What he doesn't say is "The Moon Singer is not there because I'm a traitor and I helped steal her!" What he does suggest is, "How about just a nice proper burial under a tree or something?"

"Certainly not. I will row him out to the open sea, in plain view of that magnificent clipper ship. Ishtar always wanted to be buried at sea. You wouldn't deny a dead man his final wish, would you, Judiah?"

"Oh, no, no. Of course not. I just mean that the beach is too far. Let us take him to the cove on the north side," Judiah's mouth just keeps spewing out solicitous overtures of accommodation, one sentence running into the other. "It's much closer. In fact, I'll go and fetch the dinghy from the beach and have it ready for you. I will even light some torches, as a tribute to Ishtar."

"Oh, Judiah, you are a good friend. The cove it shall be. It was one of Ishtar's favorite places." Dorinda gives him a cursory embrace. Judiah exhales in relief.

An hour later, as Dorinda requested, Judiah returns to Ishtar's cave to assist Dorinda with the burial. He and Dorinda lift the canvas bag that holds Ishtar's dead body and place it in the dinghy that Judiah brought to the cove.

"Thank you, Judiah. I will do the rest alone. I wish to say farewell to my friend in private."

"Of course, Dorinda. I understand."

Dorinda climbs into the dinghy and Judiah pushes it far enough into the water that she can enable the oars. Slowly, she rows the boat away from the shore as Judiah watches, giving a curt wave of acknowledgment now and again. Once Dorinda is past the breakers, she sees Judiah rush from the beach.

"Only a few more yards, my friend, and you will be swimming with the fishes," Dorinda says with a wry humor.

"Hurry up. It's hot as blazes in here," Ishtar complains from inside the bag.

"Well, stick your face out and breathe the air. No one can see you now."

Ishtar's face peeks out. He breathes in a grateful breath of fresh, sea air. Contented, he then inquires after Judiah. "Do you think he fell for it?"

"You were very convincing. I almost thought you were dead myself." Dorinda laughs heartily. "I only hope you can swim to the Moon Singer without truly having a heart attack."

"Desire shall be my driving force."

"Better you should have webbed feet," Dorinda quips.

Dorinda continues to row for a while. The water is smooth and calm, the only sound heard is the dipping and splashing of the oars. "I think we are far enough away from the cove," she informs Ishtar. "Thanks to Judiah, the poor stupid fool, you are now even closer to where the Moon Singer is anchored. But you must still swim 200 yards to the east."

She rotates the oars out of the water and sets them down inside the dinghy. "Let me loosen the strings on the bag. Get ready now. I'm going to push you out of the boat."

Dorinda struggles to lift Ishtar out of the dinghy and nearly falls overboard herself when Ishtar's bulk hits the water. A rope tied to the oar braces keeps the bag from sinking. Soon, Ishtar is free of the canvas bag and begins to swim smoothly away.

Dorinda watches his every move, silently praying. "Pace yourself, Ishtar. Pace yourself. Do not make even one splash."

Nineteen

"You were ordered not to come here again until I called for you."

An angry Jaycina sharply admonishes Judiah, who is breathless from his quick jog from the cove to the Palace. But he carelessly ignores her disapproval.

"Yes, High Priestess. I know. But this could not wait. I have most urgent news."

With an impatient wave of her hand, she gives him an opening. "Get on with it, then."

Judiah's news is blunt and without embellishment. "Ishtar is dead."

"What?" Jaycina's movement from sitting to standing is so swift and powerful that she nearly tips over her weighty, elaborately carved imperial chair. "You bungling idiot!"

"It's not my doing," Judiah defends himself. "He had a seizure right before my eyes. His heart gave out. He died almost instantly."

"Do you realize what this means?" Jaycina's eyes flash hotter than Judiah had ever seen them, and his boldness begins to melt into sweaty palms. "If Saliana discovers her father is dead, she will cease to sing. This will have grave implications for our Great Serpent Ruler."

"Yes, grave indeed, grave indeed. But, Jaycina, it could have fortuitous implications for you."

Her temper now under control, Jaycina sits down again, but alert like a panther waiting to spring at the slightest provocation. "Meaning?"

"Is it not true that you, High Priestess, are truly the ruler of this Palace, indeed of all the Island? You have all the responsibility while the Glass Snake reaps the rewards."

"I warn you, Judiah. Watch your tongue."

"May it be cut out if I displease you, High Priestess, but was it not you who convinced Ishtar and the Islanders to build this magnificent Palace? And was it not you who shrewdly relocated the Moon Singer out of range of the Glass Volcano, rendering the ship's crystal energy totally useless?" Judiah gushes with barely a breath. He's on a roll of sycophancy, his sole purpose to disarm Jaycina into finally giving him his due.

"True, you have unimpeachable authority over all the activities of the Palace, but think of the eternal glory you could have as ruler of the Prism Palace if -" Now he fires the winning rejoinder. " - if the Mighty Glass Snake were dead!" Judiah involuntarily clamps his hands over his mouth and winces, as though realizing he has gone too far and should bite his tongue.

A silent pause from Jaycina as she considers him and his revelation. Then, she says softly, "But he is invincible, Judiah."

"Only if Saliana sings. But if she were to learn that her father is dead, her music would cease. And the Glass Snake would be vulnerable. He could then be easily - *killed*." The word squeaks out. Judiah clears his throat. "*Ahem* - easily killed."

"And who would be brave enough to slay the Glass Snake? You, my loyal Judiah?" Jaycina nearly croons this suggestion through pursed lips.

"Me? Uh - well - yes, for you, High Priestess, I could." Then mumbles the last, "But only if he was very weak and feeble."

"Once again, you have proven your loyalty to me, Judiah. And have surprised me with your courage. You shall be justly rewarded." Jaycina claps her hands to summon two of her attendants. They enter and bow to her. "Take Judiah to the Temple Gallery and prepare him for a celebration in his honor, which shall commence tomorrow morning."

"Uh - thank you, High Priestess," Judiah says, with dubious gratitude. "It is my humble pleasure to serve you." Judiah bows to her several times and backs out of the room, an attendant with a firm grip on each of his elbows.

"The pleasure," Jaycina purrs deliciously, "is all mine, Judiah. All mine."

Twenty

Fretful, Saliana paces back and forth in her chamber. The Glass Snake roars impatiently, but Saliana stamps her foot defiantly.

"No! No, I will not sing anymore!" she shouts. Then in a hushed tone, "Oh, David, David. Where are you? Please come back and take me home."

"You mustn't upset yourself, my dear. It is not good for the voice."

Saliana spins on her heels to face the High Priestess who has unexpectedly appeared in the doorway. "What are you doing here?"

"Paying you a much overdue visit, my sweet. I fear I have neglected you. Is that why you refuse to sing this evening?"

"I shall never sing again." Saliana crosses her arms and sets her jaw stubbornly. What's the point? I'm still a prisoner, separated from my friends, never to see my father. Why should I sing?"

"When one has a great gift such as yours, how can you deprive the world? It is your duty, your obligation to use this gift."

"My gift was meant to uplift the faithful, not to give power to the greedy."

"The giving should be unconditional," Jaycina says, patronizingly, then recants with measured empathy. "But I can see your point. I suspect the real reason for your distress is your friend, David Nickerson."

"How did you know about - I mean, I don't know what you're talking about."

"Come, come, now," Jaycina says, meanness creeping back into her approach. "You know perfectly well that nothing escapes me. You believe he is here to rescue you. True?"

Saliana's voice trembles as she makes a brave attempt to stand up to Jaycina. "And what if he is? Will you keep him a prisoner just like me?"

"There is no need. David Nickerson is free to go any time he so desires. I, in fact, offered him his freedom, and yours, but he rejected it."

Saliana considers the High Priestess carefully. Jaycina is a master at switching her remarks from caustic to rueful, a technique Saliana has been subjected to countless times. Nonetheless, vulnerability clouds her thinking even as she asserts, "I don't believe you."

"As you wish," Jaycina says with a shrug, then inserts the knife of doubt a little deeper. "But did he tell you his real reason for coming to the Palace?"

"His real reason?"

"Did he not mention the plight of his young sister, Sally?" Jaycina clucks her tongue meaning to chastise David's deception. "How cruel of him. She is really the one he has come to rescue, not you. That is why he rejected my offer to let both of you leave the Palace. He believes Sally is here within these walls and he will not leave without her, even if it means he must stay here forever - with me."

Stiffening her spine with her last vestige of courage, Saliana rejects this information. "David wouldn't deceive me, but you would. You lied to my father about everything, now you're lying to me, aren't you? Aren't you!"

But Saliana is fragile from months of captivity and the mind games the High Priestess plays relentlessly. Tears begin to fall down her cheeks and she cries softly. "Oh, Jaycina, why are you doing this. Please let me go. I want to see Father. Please."

"Then grant me a small request," Jaycina says, a spider enticing a fly into its web. "Sing tonight and I will arrange a visit with your father."

"Do you mean it? Or is this another trick?" Saliana is afraid to believe her, and afraid not to. "Oh, please don't lie to me about this. Please, Jaycina."

"You have my word," Jaycina says curtly. "Sing tonight and first thing tomorrow I will hold a special reunion for the two of you."

Saliana's shoulders slump and breath streams out of her as she yields. "All right. I will sing tonight. But if I don't see my father tomorrow, I truly will never sing again."

"Fair enough," Jaycina says, victorious.

Saliana sits down in front of the tower window and picks up her harp. Through the choking tears of despair she sings:

"Moon Singer - Moon Singer - take to the sea -
Fly on the wind where the sky used to be -"

* * *

Costumed in vibrant gossamer gowns, twenty royal dancing girls twirl alluringly to the exotic music of the Palace musicians. A sumptuous feast is spread out on the banquet tables, and wine flows in abundance from jug to goblet.

Jaycina is seated on the dais in her Imperial throne, and David sits next to her. He stares straight ahead, his eyes glazed over in a hypnotic trance.

On a pedestal in front of the dais is Judiah, whose expression of terror and dilated pupils betray his gay laughter. Jaycina, he has learned, is not above a cruel joke and a whimsical change of heart. Many a celebration has turned into a last supper.

Jaycina stands, the crowd is hushed. "Loyal subjects," she says, gesturing as a benevolent host. "We are here to honor one of your friends. A man who, until now, has chosen to remain anonymous while performing countless acts of fidelity for our Great Serpent Ruler. To demonstrate our gratitude, the Princess Saliana will now sing for him. This honor, until today, has been reserved only for the Glass Snake."

Judiah chokes on his drink and the wine spurts from his nose. All eyes turn as an entourage carries Saliana on a sedan chair to the center of the dais. Her entire posture speaks resignation as she holds her harp securely in her arms. But when she sees David seated next to Jaycina, she bolts upright, her harp falling helplessly to the floor.

"David. David?" Saliana beseeches him, but he doesn't respond. She studies his face, the deadly blank stare, and a wave of knowing comes over her. "Oh, David, no."

Swiftly, Jaycina points her scepter at David and a stunning flash of light spirals around him. When it dissipates, Ishtar is standing there instead. Murmurs of astonishment spread rapidly through the crowd.

Saliana's eyes stare, unbelieving. She finds her voice but it is filled with confusion, fear and hopefulness all at once. "Father? Father...is it you? Is it really you?"

"Yes, daughter. Just as Jaycina promised. Now you must sing. It is your duty to share your gift." Ishtar is stoic and his eyes do not meet his daughter's.

Judiah clasps his hands together and bites on his knuckles. Under his breath he pleads, "Don't sing, Saliana. Oh, please don't sing. Oh, I'm doomed."

"But Father, not for the Glass Snake. This is not what my gift is for."

"Its purpose is not for you to question. Sing, Saliana, so that everyone, including the Glass Snake, can revel in the infinite beauty and divine power of your music."

Ishtar's stance, like petrified wood, is not the Ishtar Saliana knows and loves. "Father why are you saying these things? Oh, Father, what have they done to you?"

Unable to control the impulse, Judiah cries out, "Don't do it, Saliana! Don't sing. It's a trick. Ishtar is dead! It was his dying wish. Don't sing!"

Saliana screams, then sobs uncontrollably, sinking pitifully back onto the chair. Jaycina gestures and her attendants immediately rush to Saliana's side. "Take her back to the Tower," she commands with disgust. When Saliana is removed, Jaycina brandishes her scepter and Ishtar is transformed back into David Nickerson.

Judiah cowers with his face in his hands, crouched down on the pedestal. He rants madly, "David is Ishtar. Ishtar is dead. Don't sing, Saliana. Don't." He peeks through his fingers only to see no sign of her. "Where is she? Where is Saliana? She was just here. Wasn't she?"

Jaycina saunters over to the babbling Judiah. "Too much wine has stimulated your idiotic imagination," she belittles him. "Saliana is secured in the Royal Tower."

"But I saw her. I did - didn't I? You told everyone she was going to sing. I could have sworn you did, didn't you?"

Jaycina angles her head and gives Judiah a sidelong glance of pouty indignation. "And spoil your celebration? Why, you insult me. But, I forgive you." She snaps back to a festive air. "I promised you a reward for your loyalty and you shall have it. Tonight. And now," she addresses the crowd with ostentation, "let the celebration continue."

On cue, the madness of music and revelry resumes.

Twenty-one

At the base of each magnificent crystal mast of the Moon Singer is a band of solid gold rings that encircles it, much like a necklace. Using a unique cutting tool that he himself designed, Ishtar cuts through a ring on each of the three masts, freeing them at the ends. He then links the three necklaces together to make one continuous chain.

Tentatively, as he has not been aboard any sailing ship in years, he climbs the perilous 15-story rope ladder to the crow's nest with one end of the lengthy chain firmly in his grip. Because the chain is pure gold, it is light enough for Ishtar to hoist as he climbs. With each sway of the ship Ishtar halts his step and grabs onto the rope ladder for balance, repeating a mantra of faith and determination to shore up his courage.

Finally Ishtar stands in the crow's nest, overlooking the vast black ocean, and fastens the end ring of the chain to another gold band surrounding the top of the mizzenmast. He then climbs the long, precarious rope stairs down to the deck. Gripping the bottom end of the gold chain, Ishtar carries it to the railing at the ship's bow. He pulls it taut and fastens it there. Stepping back to examine his handiwork, Ishtar's face registers satisfaction. The rest will be up to David.

* * *

David stirs restlessly on the stiff cot in his sleep chamber. Awakening, he tries to sit up, but his head feels as though it's been pummeled from the inside out.

"God. What a nightmare." Is his speech slurred from the grog of sleep, or has he been drugged? He isn't sure.

He tries to rise quickly, but the room whirls around him and he slumps back down onto the cot. Looking around the room, examining his strange clothes, a grim realization comes over him that he truly is in some dark and evil place, that he may never go home again, that he has failed in his mission to find Sally. He has failed himself, his family, everyone who ever believed in him. He hasn't a clue where he is, or how or why he is enmeshed in this weird scenario.

"What's happening to me? I can't believe any of this. I've made a mess of it," he ruminates sorrowfully. "I'm sorry, Dad. Oh, Sally, Sally, I'm so sorry. God, I wish Mom was here." David covers his eyes with trembling hands balled into frightened fists, and begins to cry. He is just a boy, after all, ill equipped to understand let alone prevail in this harrowing adventure.

"Don't give up now, David." A voice, reassuring, encouraging, kind. David moves his hands from his eyes and looks up to see the hologram appear. Eagerly, he sits upright on the cot.

"Dorinda! Oh, God, I was never so happy to see anyone in my life."

"And I, you. But you mustn't let Jaycina distort your reality, or make you believe you cannot accomplish what you set out to do."

"But I can't!" he rails, angry mostly at himself. "I can't do it. Ishtar was right. I didn't know what I was doing. I should never have messed with that gridwork stuff."

"Your instincts are flawless even if your knowledge is limited. You must believe that through the crystals you have the power to succeed."

"What power? The Moldavite is gone and I can't communicate with Ishtar. I'm definitely no match for Jaycina," David denigrates himself. "And I'll never find Sally, not here in this madhouse." He shakes his head ruefully. "Why did I ever let you talk me into this?"

Dorinda is sincerely contrite. "I confess, I deceived you in the beginning, David. All I wanted was Saliana's freedom and I would have done anything, used anyone, to achieve that end."

"Everybody wants something from me, but I just want to find Sally and go home."

"But things are different now, David. We are all connected - you, me, Ishtar, Saliana, and your Sally. We are one, eternally linked together."

David feels a familiarity, an awesome recognition of some unfathomable truth. "That's what Ishtar said." He holds up his hand as though to dismiss what he cannot figure out. "But I still don't know how my being here is going to help my dad get his job back, or get Sally out of her wheel chair." He winces at the irony, realizing that Sally is, at least in this bizarre nightmare, out of her wheel chair. But where?

"You have started a chain reaction and you cannot stop it now," Dorinda implores him. "You must be more clever than Jaycina, stronger than the Glass Snake -"

"I can't do that if you're not telling me the truth," David suddenly snaps, "especially about Saliana. Jaycina says her music can't make anyone immortal, that she's only a channel for a higher source."

Noticeably unsettled by this, Dorinda asks quickly, "Did she - did she say what the source was, David?"

"No. She didn't know. But she said whoever could discover it *would* be immortal. What did she mean? What is it?"

"I must go now, David," Dorinda says hastily, her image already beginning to fade. "You shan't hear from me again. Now, you must let the magic of your gleaming crystal clipper work through you."

David moves toward her desperately. "Dorinda, no! Wait. I don't understand."

"Hold the Singer in your hand, David. Listen to its song. Listen to what it's trying to tell you…" Then, she is gone.

Nearly shattered by Dorinda's disappearance, feeling more deserted than ever, David retrieves the Singer crystal from the pocket of his tunic. He holds it tightly in his hand, willing it to speak to him, to sing to him.

"Say something, please. Let me hear it. I don't know what I'm listening for. But let me be worthy to hear the mysteries you hold." With a deep sigh and a silent prayer, he listens, and listens…and listens…

* * *

Jaycina stands watch as the palace guards drag a writhing resistant Judiah to the pedestal at the mouth of the Glass Volcano. He has been dressed in a white sacrificial garment and ornamental breastplate of precious metals and gemstones. The guards stand at either side of him, each holding one of Judiah's arms to keep him from bolting free.

"Don't do this, Jaycina, please," Judiah cries, struggling fiercely. "Send me to the mines. Anything but this!"

"The mines are for peasants, Judiah." Jaycina's smile is a flash of white teeth and ruby lips. "For you, the end must be glorious."

At the far side of the Glass Volcano, the huge lodestone is moved into place. The powerful energy of the Volcano is activated, creating an arc of electrical current. Swiftly, Judiah is pulled into the air by the magnetic force of the lodestone. He hovers, screaming, over the center of the Volcano's hungry mouth.

"Jaycina, I beg of you. Can you forget how well I have served you? Will you let one minor transgression taint my record? I don't deserve to die. Think about it!"

Dragging out Judiah's agony a bit longer, Jaycina recants. "Hmm. Perhaps you are right, Judiah. I have been hasty in deciding your fate. I will, indeed, think about it." She turns to leave, but turns back a moment to hear yet another plea from Judiah.

"No! You can't leave me here. JAYCINA –" his terrified voice echoes across the valley.

Flamboyantly, the High Priestess twirls her cape closed around her and walks away, leaving Judiah dangling like a marionette in mid-air between life and death.

* * *

Feelings of peace and calm flow gently inside David. Although no great revelation has occurred, no sounding brass or flashes of insight, an inner strength shores him up and he decides to make one last valiant effort to rescue Saliana. As he slips quietly from his sleep chamber, he is amazed that no guard stands at the door. And as he retraces his steps up the spiraling staircase, no one appears to stop him.

Warily, David moves through the Palace to Saliana's chamber in the Tower, grateful that he hears no sounds indicating the Glass Snake is near. He hesitates for a moment outside Saliana's door and listens, completely enchanted by the exquisite purity of her voice. Is this the song his crystal sings? The one his heart sings? Both, he knows. Both. And each has brought him here to this place.

Remembering the urgency of the moment, he snaps alert then strides quickly through the door. Saliana turns with a start and gasps at the sight of him.

"Oh - David. I'm so glad to see you." She rushes to his side and grasps his hands, pulling them gratefully to her tear-stained face.

"Don't sing anymore, Saliana."

"But, Father said -"

"It was just a trick. That wasn't your father."

Saliana's lips quiver. "Then it's true. Father is dead."

"No. It's not true. Believe me."

Saliana swoons with relief and David's arms sweep around her to steady her. She feels strangely comfortable to him, someone he embraced long ago, or dreamed he did, hoped someday he would. In turn, she slips her arms around him, silently holding him for a moment. She steps back slightly, head tilted expectantly. Their eyes search each other's with longing, yearning, questioning. David moves closer to her waiting lips, but suddenly Saliana's eyes reflect uncertainty.

"David. You *are* David now, aren't you? Not under Jaycina's spell?"

David shakes his head, also feeling doubtful about his state of mind. "No. I think I've come to my senses. But I don't know what will happen if I encounter Jaycina again." He takes a firm hold of Saliana's hand. "Come on," he says, leading her to the door. "We don't have much time."

"Where are we going?"

"Home."

Twenty-two

Following the blue mirrors as Ishtar had told him to do, David leads Saliana through the winding, seemingly endless Palace corridors. The sonorous chanting, that so intrigued David earlier, again resounds through the walls, the mantras enveloping him with their primitive urgings. With an overwhelming desire to succumb to their enticements, David halts his step. Yearning fills him, and a yielding expression crosses his face. He lets Saliana's hand slip from his and makes a slow move away from her.

Alarmed, Saliana cries out. "Come back, David. Come back!" The strong tone of her voice strikes a protective nerve and David tenses his body, fighting the impulse to follow the chanting and to be drawn into its womb of mystery and magic.

David summons his inner strength and orders her sharply, "Just keep moving." Saliana grasps David's hand with both of hers as they proceed further along. Nearing Jaycina's chamber, an eerie shimmering presence dances in front of them. Saliana lets out a small cry and shields herself behind David's shoulder.

"What is that, David? It's like a mirage or something."

"That's just what it is. Hurry past," David urges her as beads of perspiration dot his face. "Where is that damn staircase?"

They scurry along as a haunting, lilting voice echoes David's name. David grits his teeth and clenches his fist resisting, resisting, shutting out the enticement.

"David," the voice intones seductively. "It's Jaycina. You hear me, don't you?" "No! I won't listen!" *Why can't I be deaf now?* David wonders desperately.

Jaycina's voice reverberates from high and low, from far and near, from every nook and cranny, but David presses on valiantly until he finds the hidden staircase.

"We're here." David's voice breaks under the stress. "It's the hidden stairs your father told me about. Come on."

But Saliana hesitates a moment and looks back up the corridor. She freezes when she sees the High Priestess standing but a few feet away. Suddenly, a door slides across their path, closing off the staircase to freedom. David pushes on it with all his might, but it doesn't budge.

"No, Jaycina," David hisses vehemently through clenched teeth, "not this time. We're leaving and you can't stop us."

"Of course, I cannot stop you, David. You are free to go anytime."

"Oh, sure. What are we supposed to do, just walk through this door?"

"The door will open easily if you truly want to leave. So, obviously you wish to stay and learn more of the wonders of the Prism Palace."

"I've seen all I want to see of you and that monster you worship. The two of you deserve each other."

At her manipulative best Jaycina proclaims, "The Prism Palace is just the beginning for us, David. Soon there will be the temples of healing and science that Ishtar dreamed of."

"All monuments to lies and greed, built on the blood and tears of helpless people," Saliana injects bitterly, coming out from behind David's protection.

"You misunderstand my intentions," Jaycina replies, with carefully disguised condescension. "I only wanted to give the Islanders a chance to live a purposeful life, to save them from their primitive existence of idleness and useless fantasies."

"You're the one who lives in a fantasy, Jaycina," David sneers, "to think I would stay here in this crazy world with someone like you."

Jaycina's shrill laughter sends shivers through David's body, then her words pierce his heart like a knife. "You are so naive, my David. Is your world any different? Lies and greed have all but destroyed your own father. Did he not choose his work above all else, killing your mother and crippling your sister in the process?"

"No!" David screams, clutching his stomach which feels like it's being ripped out. Saliana is taken aback at his outburst and stands frozen in shock.

"It's not true. It's because of Fischbacher, that slave driver, that – *snake*. And I'll get even if it's the last thing I do!" David lunges at Jaycina threateningly, but his hands slip right through her. She is there, but untouchable, like a ghost, an illusion, an elusive fragment of a dream.

"The only way to overthrow the powerful is with greater power, the kind of power I can give you," Jaycina baits him. "Isn't that why you are here?"

Why am I here? David asks himself the unanswerable question, wondering if he will ever comprehend this odd interplay of his life with the lives of Ishtar, Saliana and, most of all, Jaycina. *What is it I'm trying to prove, anyway?*

"But it takes time, David," Jaycina continues to cajole him. "And if Saliana will sing for all of us, we will have the time. We will all be immortal, you and I as well as the great Serpent Ruler."

"Immortal? That's an even bigger lie," David confronts her. "You told me yourself Saliana's music can't make anyone immortal."

Jaycina circles Saliana like a hungry tiger stalking her prey. "But she holds the key. Somewhere in her song is the answer to all things. And I MUST HAVE IT!" Jaycina is shrieking now, venting an anger that springs up like a geyser of resentment finally bursting free. Stark terror emblazons Saliana's eyes and she places a protective hand over the Rose Crystal Pendant.

Jaycina rails on. "For a thousand lifetimes I have subjugated myself to kings and conquerors, denied the status that I truly deserve, that is my birthright. The Crystal of Wisdom is rightfully mine," she insists, not knowing she speaks of the singer David carries in his tunic. "I will find it and I will reclaim it, if I have to crush everyone in my path."

David moves between Jaycina and Saliana, guarding Saliana from this madwoman who stands before them. "Even me?" he challenges the High Priestess. David's forthright stare triggers something in Jaycina, and she becomes quiescent, yet her eyes are strangely pleading.

"No, David. Not you. We are friends, you and I. Don't you see? I wasn't always corrupt. I have been corrupted by *them*. I have had to play the game their way to

survive." Jaycina grabs David's arm fervently. "But survival is not enough. I want to live again, David. I want to live again to fulfill my destiny as I choose."

David's heart swirls with a tidepool of confusing emotions, the same conflict he felt when he confronted Janice Cole. Once she had been his friend, someone he could trust. But she, too, was corrupted, by Nathan Fischbacher at the expense of her own free will and dignity. The remembrance of Janice's intent to marry Nathan Fischbacher raises his hackles and any ambiguity of emotion dissolves.

"You can stay dead for all I care." David pulls his arm fiercely away from Jaycina and begins to lead Saliana away. *Stay dead? Why did I say that?* David wonders why he didn't say *drop* dead.

"Wait, please, David." In her desperation, Jaycina's approach transforms to an appealing softness. "What about Sally? I will give you your Sally if you will leave Saliana with me."

David halts and turns to Jaycina. "You don't know where Sally is. It's another one of your tricks."

"Look, David. Look into my eyes and see. See your Sally."

Belligerently, David strides over to Jaycina and stands inches from her. He peers deeply into her glistening black eyes, believing he will see nothing save for her piercing glance. But, magically, there she is. Sally - laughing and happy, just as she used to be. She whirls and dances gracefully to a merry waltz like a princess, just like a princess...

"Sally - Sally -" David whispers. He swallows the thick lump that grows in his throat. Jaycina extends her hand invitingly. David reaches out and takes it in his own. Jaycina's smile emits a look of conquest.

Now, David. The voice in his head urges him. Ishtar's voice. *Now. You know what you must do.*

In a remarkably deft move, David pulls the diamond ring from Jaycina's finger and forces the pyramid ring on in its place. Taken completely by surprise, Jaycina struggles to remove the ring, but it will not come off.

"No! No! It's can't be! It can't be!" Jaycina wails. Anger, disbelief, and terror intermingle in her eyes and cries of protest. Mystifyingly, Jaycina transforms into the formidable and awe-inspiring form of the Glass Snake, then back to Jaycina again. She is a shimmering wave of color, she is smoke and fire, she is passion and fury, darkness and light. She is everything real and yet fantastic, everything imaginable but inconceivable.

David and Saliana recoil in horror and rush to the hidden staircase. Amazingly, the barricading door opens wide and they pass through the portal.

"What did you do to her?" Saliana asks, breathless as they descend the dozens of marble steps.

"I exchanged rings - put on the one your father gave me. He said it would make her change."

"That was an understatement."

"She was supposed to change for the better."

At last, they reach the bottom of the stairs, then stop short of the archway.

"Wait," David cautions her. "Let me see what's out there." He passes through the archway, then quickly returns. "It's the way out, to the front of the Palace. It's clear."

David and Saliana run, their feet barely touching the ground beneath them, the Prism Palace illuminating their way in the darkness. As they approach the perimeter of the Palace grounds, Saliana stops abruptly. Before them is Judiah, hovering over the mouth of the Glass Volcano. He is conscious but weak.

"Holy cow," David exclaims.

"David - help me - help - me -" Judiah whimpers.

Saliana is frantic. "What do we do!"

"I don't know," David says, completely at a loss.

With surprising alertness, Judiah begins screaming. "He's coming. He's coming."

Saliana and David turn to see the Glass Snake thundering across the Palace grounds toward them. He moves quickly on massive clawed feet, despite the stubby thickness of his legs. His powerful gait shakes the ground, nearly knocking David and Saliana off their balance. They scramble to the pedestal at the mouth of the Volcano and climb up on it. The Snake is mere yards away, his wild eyes two red mirrors of doom. Saliana shrieks hysterically.

David is unexpectedly struck with a sharp, searing pain in his ear and he reaches up to hold it. The pain then turns into an unbearable ringing and David pulls his hearing aid out, cutting off all the sounds of panic that surround him. As he does so, the din becomes a hum, then a soothing hush, like the tranquil ebb and flow of the ocean tides he loves so much. Immersed in this secure cocoon, David realizes instinctively what he must do and reaches into his tunic for the Singer crystal. He holds it high, like a cross of "good" opposing the forces of evil.

Instantly, the Singer is ignited with the crackling energy emanating from the Glass Volcano and emits a dazzling, prismatic spray of multi-colored light, which then emblazons the Star of David on David's tunic.

"His tail, David. Cut off his tail and he will die!" Judiah yells.

David points the Singer toward the Snake's tail and the little crystal clipper spews out a hail of incendiary sparks. The Snake's scaly tail explodes into a million pieces, sending fragments of shattering multi-colored glass into the sky like a Fourth of July fireworks display. The Snake roars violently, one final gasp for life before the instant of death, then collapses in a thunderous heap.

In the explosion, a glorious burst of light hurtles through the sky like a meteor toward the Moon Singer. The energy hits the gallant clipper ship's railing, slithers along the conduit Ishtar fashioned from the gold rings, and connects to the clipper's mizzenmast full force. Her sails burst open and, regaining full power, the Moon Singer begins to glide along on the water.

Ishtar runs up and down the main deck, whooping victoriously, as a misty spray of water washes away his grateful tears. "You did it, David! You did it. You remembered, my boy. You remembered."

Twenty-three

Like a mighty beast slain by a hunter's shot, the Glass Snake lies lifeless on the Palace grounds. David and Saliana stand back, shuddering in awe at the events that have just occurred. Then, hesitantly, they move in unison toward the beast to fully take in its charred image, but it disintegrates into a gaseous fog. When it clears, Jaycina stands in the beast's place.

She has, indeed, changed. No more blood-red robe, ostentatious headdress, garish makeup or razor-like fingernails. This Jaycina wears a simple white sheath and a gracefully soft green cape. Her raven hair is braided gently with gold ribbons. And on her finger, the clear pyramid stone has turned the deep blue of a summer evening's sky.

Do David's eyes deceive him still? She is Jaycina, but is she? Saliana clings to David and he, in turn, holds fast to her.

"Don't be afraid, Saliana," Jaycina says in a silken voice. "I'm not the Jaycina you once knew."

"Which Jaycina are you now?" David asks suspiciously. "What kind of trick is this?

"No more tricks, my brave David Nickerson. No more deceit."

She sounds sincere, reassuring, but David is not quite ready to accept her transformation. "How do we know you're not lying again?"

Jaycina nods with understanding. "Ask me anything and it shall be granted."

"Judiah," David says, motioning to the poor wretch suspended overhead. "Save him from the volcano."

"As you wish." Jaycina extends her hand and points the pyramid ring toward the Volcano. Instantly, the huge arc of electrical charges disappears. Falling, Judiah screams, but a surge of magnetic power pulls him swiftly toward the lodestone. Arms and legs spread-eagle, Judiah lands forcefully on the lodestone, then slithers to the ground.

"Judiah will need care, but he will live," Jaycina observes.

"Not that he deserves it, the weasel," Saliana comments with surprising candor.

"Have you another request, David?" Jaycina asks.

"Yes. Let Saliana and the Islanders go free."

"Their freedom is not mine to give -"

"I thought so," David jumps in sharply.

Jaycina continues, unperturbed, "They have but to believe they are free and be slaves no more. One day you will understand. And perhaps one day you will also find it in your heart to forgive." She bows graciously to David and Saliana, then turns and walks nobly back toward the Palace, her image dissipating into the ether.

Twenty-four

The morning sun is a warm glow in an Azure blue sky as David and Saliana cross over the Palace boundary and enter the dense forest of the Island. Lush groves have replaced the bramble, and mirrored pools of water give sanctuary to a plethora of birds and fish. Peacocks strut in rainbow-colored grandeur across the plush, emerald green carpets of grass.

"If I didn't know better, I'd say this was Paradise," David says, awed by the miracle that turned the dark and foreboding island into an ethereal and vital wonderland.

"Paradise is where you are happiest, David," Saliana says. "I suspect your Paradise lies back home with your family, and your Sally."

David is wistful. "Yes, Sally. Will I ever find her, Saliana?"

"She is very close, David. Very close."

David is silent a moment, then asks a question that has been burning inside him. "Is it true, Saliana? Can your music really give someone the gift of immortality?"

Saliana's eyes are filled with tenderness as she answers, "Only faith and love can give us eternal life, David. My music is the way I express faith and love to all who desire to listen." She removes the Rose Crystal pendant from her neck and folds it into David's hand with her own. "For your Sally, when you find her."

David leans forward to kiss her and she turns her face up to his invitingly. But their sweet union is interrupted by the shouts of an excited Ishtar running toward them.

"Saliana! Saliana," Ishtar calls eagerly, gratefully, breathlessly.

"Father!" Saliana runs to Ishtar, embraces him, and weeps with him in happiness.

"Oh, dear daughter, I feared I might never see you again."

"Father, did you have so little faith?"

"I am ashamed to confess it faltered, child, it faltered."

"Ishtar. I'm so glad you're all right," David greets him fondly. Ishtar throws his arms around David in a bearish, fatherly hug. "My boy, I shall be forever grateful, forever in your debt."

"You don't owe me anything, Ishtar. But maybe you can help me find the Moon Singer."

"Find her?" Ishtar's laughs heartily. "David, my boy, she is not only found, but in full power, ready to set sail. Come, I'll show you."

Quickly, the trio makes their way to the Island beach. The Moon Singer, in all her splendor, stands proud atop the tranquil ocean.

Ishtar gestures grandly toward the clipper ship. "There she is, David. Ready and waiting."

David is ecstatic, but confused. "But, how did you get her moving? There was no power."

"Not I, David. You did it. You and your little Singer crystal. I knew if you could get that ring on Jaycina's finger, everything would fall into place like a row of dominoes. I knew you'd remember the power that got you here in the first place, and use it well. When you aligned the Singer to the Volcano's energy flow - well, you should have seen it, my boy. An explosion of light like a flotilla of angels from heaven. In an instant, the Moon Singer regained her full power and order was restored to the universe."

"And killed the Glass Snake," David surmises.

"*Because* the Glass Snake was killed," Ishtar explains. "The Snake was created by Jaycina's immoral use of the knowledge she possessed. You and your Singer restored wisdom and truth to the island, and evil is powerless in the light of Truth, my boy."

"What will you and Saliana do now, Ishtar?"

Ishtar places his arm lovingly around Saliana's shoulder. "Try to rebuild our lives. Perhaps try to rebuild the City of Light for its true purpose. And perhaps this time Jaycina will unite with us instead of against us."

Recalling the vision of Jaycina disappearing into nothingness, David questions Ishtar, "But how can she? Saliana and I both saw her completely fade away as though she never existed, like she was dead."

"In a manner of speaking, she did die," Ishtar says. "But if she truly atones for her past actions she will come back again."

Saliana kisses David's cheek. "Good-bye, David. Your voyage home will be peaceful and all your dreams will come true."

"Good-bye, Saliana. I'll never forget you."

"You had better not," she says, with a warm laugh.

David finds the clipper's dinghy on the beach and pushes it into the water. He jumps in and begins to row, with half-reluctant and half-determined strokes, to the Moon Singer. Ishtar and Saliana wave farewell from the shore. David waves back as bittersweet tears trickle down his face. He is going home, enriched by new friendships, but going home without Sally.

"Do you think David really knows the true power of his little Singer crystal, Father, that it was fashioned from the masthead of the Moon Singer?"

"No, not yet," Ishtar replies. "But if he remembers what has happened here, some day he will understand why the Moon Singer came into his possession."

"I think he will use the knowledge well," Saliana says with certainty.

"Yes. But if it should fall into the wrong hands once he is back in his own world…"

"It won't, Father. You see, I gave David my Rose Crystal pendant."

"Containing the music codes of the trinity?"

"Yes. The Crystal of Wisdom activated by the Rose Crystal's Love results in Truth - the only power that David will ever need in this or any world."

"You are very unselfish, my daughter. And very wise. Now let us pray he acquires the third sacred artifact as well, the one that will let him unlock the codes."

"If he has the courage to follow his destiny, he will."

Steadily, the Moon Singer sails away, her white sails bursting full in the wind, her crystal masts glistening in the sun. David slips his hand into his vest pocket and retrieves the note Ishtar had given him just before he left the Island. He reads it with fascination:

"You asked how I knew, living in what appears to be a primitive society, about such things as electronics and forms of energy that only modern man can know of. How did the ancient Egyptians know about advanced engineering and architectural concepts, or the Atlantians progress to a sophisticated civilization worthy of legend and fascination.

"It is because nothing is new under the sun, not even knowledge. When we discover new facts, skills, and tools today, we are not just learning from our past but we are also remembering our future. For the past, present and future are all one."

As David stands at the stern, an enormous wave rolls up and crests under the Moon Singer. The mystical ship takes flight, higher and higher into the endless reaches of the universe, and the deep blue ocean below becomes a slick sea of glass once again. Under its transparent reflection, the Island grows smaller and disappears, just as David's hometown did at the start of his voyage.

"I'll be back," David vows, not knowing when or how, but knowing all the same.

Like an angel's serenade, Saliana's song echos all around, guiding David's voyage home on the Crystal Clipper:

"I know a place where the Moon Riders sail

On a translucent river of diamonds and pearls.

They journey through time,

Until time ceases moving,

Then float gently home on the soft wings of twilight.

Moon Singer, Moon Singer, take to the sea,

Fly on the wind where the sky used to be.

Moon Singer, Moon Singer, take me along.

Keep me safe in your light till I find my way home."

Twenty-five

Port Avalon

Harry Judd shifts uncomfortably on his feet, confronted by an authoritative Janice Cole requesting the official files for the sale of Fischbacher Shipping, Inc.

"I don't know, Miss Cole. I'm really not permitted to turn over any files to outside parties on any transaction."

"I'm hardly an outside party, Harry. I'm not only Nathan's fiancée, I am his executive assistant with a seat on the Board." Janice leans in toward him, speaking in a conspiratorial tone. "It wouldn't do to have any mistakes in these files when David Nickerson comes back again with his lawyers, would it?"

Judd retains his haughty stance, but his forehead is clammy with nervous sweat. "Let them come. I have nothing to hide. My hands are clean."

"I want to be sure the *files* are clean, for Nathan's sake, and for yours. You understand, don't you, Harry? I promise I'll have them back to you in a few hours. And no one will know we had this little chat, will they?"

Judd draws himself up officiously. Recalcitrant at first, then yielding to the inevitable, he retrieves the file from his cabinet. He hands it rudely to Janice.

"Oh, and I'll take the other file, too, Harry. The one in your personal desk drawer?"

Judd opens his mouth to protest, but changes his mind. He stomps to his desk, pulls the file folder from the drawer and thrusts it at her. Janice snaps her briefcase closed with the files safely inside.

"Thank you, Harry. I'll put in a good word for you with Nathan."

Back in her office, Janice scrutinizes every word, every clause in the sale papers, noticeably disturbed by what she sees. With each new revelation, she places her hand up to her mouth, her throat, her heart, as if to hold back the shock. After a long, intense moment of contemplation, she swivels around in her chair and gazes intently at Nathan's portrait on the wall.

"Oh, Nathan. How could you be so insidious, and yet so seductive? And how could I have been so blind?"

Janice holds up her hand and studies her diamond engagement ring. She removes it carefully and places it in a small *cloisonné* dish on her desk. With determination to stem the flow of tears, Janice begins to work on the files.

When early morning sun at last filters through the vertical blinds, Janice turns off the desk lamp. She heaves a sigh and leans back wearily in her chair. Just then, Nathan enters the office and is startled to find her already at work at her desk.

"God, Jan. What are you doing here so early? You look like – didn't you sleep well?"

"Actually, Nathan, I didn't sleep at all. I've been working all night on a rather important business deal."

Nathan's brows form parentheses around suspicious eyes. "What deal?"

"Let's talk about it in your office. I think you'd better be sitting down for this."

Nathan shrugs dismissively and turns on his heels, grumbling, "I don't know what this is about, but let's do it later."

Janice follows him into his office and slams the door closed. "We'll do it now, Nathan. It's later than you think."

Registering surprise at her demand, Nathan slowly lowers himself into his chair.

"Nathan, why do you want to marry me?"

"Oh, for Pete's – is that what this is about?" He laughs with a semblance of relief. "Because I love you. You know that." The words are devoid of emotion.

"You love *me*, or my stock options?"

"Is this some sort of pre-wedding jitters? I'd never expect you to act so immaturely, Jan, like a blushing bride. Not at your age."

"Thank you for reminding me that I'm old enough to know better. I had forgotten. I've been just like a dependent little girl. First on my father who sheltered me from all the realities of life. Then, dependent on you to take care of the business my family built and nurtured for more than a century, instead of having the courage to run it myself."

"Run this business?" Nathan smirks, and laughs derisively. "You're a bright girl, Janice, but hardly the kind of woman who could manage a worldwide industry."

"You mean I'm not like you, Nathan? A liar, a cheat, a fraud, a stock manipulator?"

Nathan's face turns gray, as though all the blood has been drained from his body. "What are you talking about?"

"This." Janice thrusts a file folder at him. "This is what I'm talking about."

Nathan's jaw stiffens and the blood returns to his face in a fury. "Where did you get this?"

"From your slimy cohort, Harry Judd. I overheard the two of you talking when you ordered Judd to hide the real file from David Nickerson, so he wouldn't know the truth about the sale."

"What truth?" Nathan hedges. "It's a perfectly valid sale. None of that kid's business anyway."

"And none of mine? Did you really think you could get away with it, Nathan? How long do you think it would be before I discovered that you used my stock options to perpetrate a phony deal?"

"You see what I mean, Jan? You're just not equipped to handle the intricacies of business. Once we're married, your stock options are as good as mine. So, no harm done."

Janice throws her head back and emits a low growl of consternation. "You are amazing, Nathan. Truly amazing. How convenient you post-dated the sale just one day after our wedding was to take place."

"What do you mean *was* to take place?"

"Let's make a deal, Nathan." Janice hands him another file folder. "Let's open file Number Two."

Twenty-six

The soothing sound of distant thunder is all that remains of the afternoon storm. Low lying clouds begin to break up, welcoming the gradual return of the sun.

"David. David - please wake up, David." Sally cradles her brother's head in her lap and rubs his face, trying to rouse him.

Finally, David opens his eyes. "Holy cow. What happened?"

"I think you were struck by lightning, a huge bolt of lightning." Sally is still shaken by the experience. "It struck your crystals and then you fell over. I thought you were dead."

David raises up on one elbow and shakes his head to clear it. "How long was I out?"

"For a few minutes. I'm not sure. The storm came and went so fast it didn't seem real." Sally helps David stand up and brushes sand from his clothes.

"If you think the storm was unreal," David begins, "wait till I tell you about..." Then he stops, dumbstruck at this vision of his sister before him. "My God! Sally - you're standing. You're standing! How?"

Sally is as befuddled as David. "I don't know. I was in my chair next to you and when I saw you get hurt all I could think of was - Oh, David, I couldn't stand it if anything happened to you."

David hugs her fiercely, feeling their mutual sibling devotion. "Me, too, Sal. Me, too. But you can walk now. You can walk."

He spins her around and their joyous laughter echoes across the bay. When he sets her down, David notices the Rose Crystal pendant around Sally's neck. It's the pendant that Saliana had given him before he left the Island.

* * *

"You may all come in now." His examination completed, the Nickerson family doctor snaps his medical bag closed as Isaac, Dorothy and David enter Sally's bedroom. David sits on the bed next to his sister and holds her hand.

"I can't explain it, Isaac," Dr. McMillan says, still baffled. "She seems perfectly fine. Oh, just a little weak, but all her mobility seems to have returned. It might only be temporary, but it surely gives us hope for a full recovery."

Isaac's voice trembles with gratitude, "It's a miracle. Nothing less than a miracle."

Dr. McMillan nods in agreement. "Sometimes a shock produces results that medicine just can't explain."

"Miracle is as good an explanation as any I can think of," Dorothy chimes in, obviously tickled pink.

"I'll get it, Dad," David offers when the front door bell rings.

But Dorothy motions for him to stay put, that she will answer it. In their excitement over Sally's recovery, no one notices that David actually heard the doorbell.

"You get a lot of rest, young lady," the doctor gives Sally a firm order. "Tomorrow we'll put you through some real tests, maybe see if you can still jitterbug like you used to."

Sally pokes fun at him playfully. "Oh, Doctor, nobody jitterbugs anymore."

"Well, maybe it's time they did," he says with a wink. He and Isaac leave the room discussing the next steps he will take on Sally's case.

"Sally, this has got to be the happiest day of my life," David says. "Dad's right. It's a miracle."

"You did it, David. You made it happen."

"Me? How could I?"

"Your crystals, David. I know it was the magic of your crystals on the sand."

"Some magician I am. I get hit by lightning and miss the whole thing."

"But I didn't." Sally lowers her voice to a whisper. "Something else happened after the lightning struck. I couldn't tell Dad. He'd think I was crazy or something. But I know you'll understand."

"What is it, Sal? What did you see?"

"There was this face - a woman's face. She looked like a gypsy or a fortune teller or something. Only she wasn't really there. It was more like I could see right through her, like a ghost or –"

"Like a hologram?"

"Yes. That's it. And she had this crystal ball. She kept calling my name and, this was really weird - she looked just like Aunt Dorothy. Remember when she dressed up and told fortunes at the Halloween Party?" David nods. "Like that. Well, then the gypsy disappeared and the next thing I remember I was out of my wheelchair and kneeling on the sand next to you. I think you conjured her up with the crystals, and she must have had some mystical powers that made me walk again."

David is silent, taking it all in.

"Do you think I'm crazy, David?"

David laughs and squeezes his sister's hand. "If you're crazy, Sally, then we both are. Two loony tunes."

Sally looks closely at the side of her brother's head. "Where is your hearing aid? How can you hear without it?"

"My hearing aid?" The last he saw it, he had pulled it out just before killing the Glass Snake. "Oh, it was dirty, so I took it out," he says, evasively. "Besides, you know what a champion 'lipper' I am."

"Undisputed champ," Sally praises him. "But you heard Dad, too, and the doctor. You weren't reading their lips. And you heard the doorbell. How?" Her eyes widen. "Maybe it's another miracle, David."

"Maybe. But don't tell anyone just yet. One miracle a day is all this family can handle."

Janice Cole settles comfortably on the living room sofa and accepts the cup of tea Dorothy serves her. "I hope I'm not intruding on your family, Isaac, but I was so thrilled to hear about Sally. I just had to come by."

"It's very considerate of you, Janice," Isaac says affably.

David enters the room whistling, but stops short when he sees Janice. She greets him amiably.

"David. I'm so happy about Sally."

David's response is curt. "Yeah. We are, too." He walks over to the fireplace and leans on the mantel, avoiding Janice's eyes.

Janice places her teacup on the table and walks over to him. "David, I'm sorry about what happened in Nathan's office the other day."

Isaac's eyebrows lift with curiosity. "What happened in Nathan's office?"

"You should be apologizing to my father, not to me," David snaps.

"Apologize to me? What for?" Isaac asks, but no one pays him any mind.

"You're right," Janice concedes, "but I knew an apology wouldn't be enough. I had to do something to stop Nathan before it was too late."

"Stop Nathan from what?" Isaac again tries to get a response.

"The only way to stop a man like Nathan Fischbacher is to crush him and break him into little pieces," David says with pure venom.

"The only way to break Nathan," Janice counters, "is to beat him at his own game, the game he calls 'strictly business.'" She turns to Isaac and explains, "Nathan lied to you about your designs, Isaac. They're magnificent, not worthless as Nathan told you. He was planning to sell them out from under you. When he told me this, I realized David had been right, only I was too blind to see."

Dorothy is signing Janice's conversation for David, and he plays along, signaling his understanding to his aunt, while hearing every startling word.

"I was so angry," Janice is saying, "and so ashamed. I decided to help David approach the new owners of the company, let them know who really created those designs and ask them to keep you on when they took over."

Isaac dismisses Janice's notion with a resigned wave of his hand. "No, Janice. I don't really care anymore. I'm up to here with it. The new owners probably aren't any less conniving and selfish than Nathan."

Janice smiles knowingly. "Oh, I don't know, Isaac. I think when you hear who the new owners are, you might change your mind."

"I doubt it."

Suddenly remembering something, David interjects. "Wait a minute. I went to the Administrator's office myself to look at the sale papers. There was no record of the new owners. How could you find out?"

"Being Nathan's assistant all these years has taught me a few things about business deals, believe me, David," Janice explains without boasting. "I overheard Nathan talking to someone over the phone, telling him not to let you find any information about the sale. I recognized the man's voice. It was Harry Judd at the City Administrator's office. I never did trust that little weasel."

David is agitated, but not surprised that Harry Judd had lied to him.

"Yes. He knew that Nathan himself bought the company and listed one of his subsidiary corporations as the buyer," Janice reveals.

Now Isaac springs up from his chair, a fire lit under him. "I can't believe it. I knew Nathan was unscrupulous, but to falsify the sale…"

"…and to sell it to one of his own corporations," Dorothy adds, just as confounded as her brother. "It doesn't make any sense."

"Yes, it's very complicated," Janice says. "And he could very easily have gotten away with it since the buying corporation is in a blind trust. No one would ever know he bought his own company at a cut rate to monopolize the stock options, fully intent on reselling it for a higher price."

"But now they will." Dorothy slaps her knees and hoots gleefully. Fischbacher is finally going to get his due. "You *are* going to report him to the authorities, aren't you Janice?"

"I thought of that, but I came up with a better idea."

David snorts cynically. "What could be better than seeing Fischbacher rot in jail?" *Except maybe to cut off his tail,* David thinks to himself, remembering the satisfying vision of the Glass Snake's demise.

"Nathan's going to jail wouldn't help your father or the other employees. But this will." Janice retrieves some papers from her purse and gives them to Isaac to read. "These contracts are iron clad and totally legal, Isaac."

Isaac scans the papers then looks up at Janice, stunned. "You? You're the new owner? How did you manage that?"

"I rewrote the sale agreement." Janice's face beams with a mixture of pride and humility. "Oh, don't worry. I have plenty of stock in the company as well as my inheritance to put in a serious bid. And the stock held by you and the other employees will solidify the transaction, if you'll all be willing to sign them over in exchange for a limited partnership agreement."

Isaac is dumbfounded, but nods enthusiastically. "Of course we will. But how in the world did you get Nathan to agree to this?"

"He called it blackmail. I called it shrewd negotiating. One shipping company in exchange for my silence."

Impressed by Janice's courageous actions, David is contrite for his attitude toward her. "Gosh, Janice. I had you all wrong. I'm sorry for everything I said. I had no right, especially to insinuate you were marrying Fischbacher for his money."

"It's all right, David. I know how devoted you are to your father and to Sally. I would have felt the same under the circumstances." She moves closer to David and takes his hand in a gesture of friendship. "Actually, I should thank you for forcing me to open my eyes. I could never have married a man whose whole life is a lie. I guess my life has been one for a long time."

David glances down at Janice's hand holding his, and the startling blue stone that sparkles on her finger. "Your ring. It's different. It's blue."

"Yes. It was my mother's ring," she says, brightening. "I thought I had lost it years ago, but it suddenly turned up. Isn't that strange?"

David grins at the irony. "Just another in a series of strange things happening."

"Well, I don't know about any of you," Isaac breaks in after a poignant silence, "but these past few days have been overwhelming. I don't know if I could stand any more surprises."

"Oh, there is just one more thing, Isaac. If you're not busy for dinner, I'd like to talk some business with you." Janice takes Isaac by the arm and gently nudges him toward the door. "There just happens to be a vice presidency that's open..."

Epilogue

It's a brisk, sunny morning as Dorothy and David walk along the wharf where David had first encountered the gypsy hologram and the Moon Singer. It hardly seems possible that such an outlandish experience could have occurred in this quiet place.

"I haven't seen such vibrancy in your father's eyes since before your mother died, rest her soul."

"He's pretty happy all right," David says. "He's finally getting recognition for his talents."

"And a little recognition from Janice Cole isn't hurting things either, if you know what I mean," Dorothy adds with a wink.

David is delighted, for more reasons than his aunt really knows. He never realized before that, deep down, he harbored feelings of resentment toward his father because of the accident. But since returning home from his voyage on the Moon Singer David has a deeper understanding and appreciation for Isaac's own inner torment. David feels renewed, re-energized, like his crystals after being cleansed in the ocean. Somehow, so many things that had previously been clouded by fear and doubt were now amazingly clear. Yet, oddly, he also has a mountain of new questions that need to be answered.

Where had he actually gone? And how did he get there? If he had been transported to the Island by accident, could he ever return? Would he ever sail the Moon Singer again? Was his journey a kind of time travel? A past life experience? Everyone he had encountered on the Island looked so much like the people he knew at home in Port Avalon, or gave him the same feeling of familiarity.

If the past, present and future are all one, as Ishtar told him, and if there truly is an eternal connection between souls as Dorinda had said, then on some level Dad, Sally, Aunt Dorothy, Janice - they've all had the same experience. *Why do I remember and they don't? Why did I relive it now? And where was Mom? Will I see her again in some strange other world?*

There was one thing he knew for certain: his adventure hadn't been a dream. Oh, it was as fantastic as any dream he had ever had, but it wasn't surreal or disjointed. Everything flowed and made sense in its context. And its texture was different. It didn't have that fuzzy, two-dimensional quality that dreams have. It had depth and a rich substance, as real as it felt now walking on the pier with his Aunt Dorothy, breathing in the clean, invigorating sea air. The sea. He finally realized why his family, for centuries, had loved it so, why they still do.

"So, where are you off to next, Aunt Dorothy? Some new exotic place?"

"Heaven's, no. I've traveled far and wide enough in my lifetime. I'm going to stay put for awhile, visit with my favorite nephew." She slips her arm around his affectionately. "And I plan to do some sailing and a lot of fishing. That's why I bought this." Dorothy motions to a sleek white sloop docked at the end of the wharf. "Isn't she a beauty?"

David quickens his step toward the boat. "Holy cow! She sure is. What do you call her?"

Dorothy catches up to him. "Well, I haven't christened her yet. You know, she kind of reminds me of your little Singer crystal. Think there's a name for her? The Singer?"

David ponders a minute, then casts out an idea. "What do you think of Moon Singer?"

"Moon Singer? Hmm. That's catchy. Where did you come up with a name like that?"

"Aunt Dorothy - there's something I've been wanting to tell you about that crystal you gave me."

Perhaps it's the reflection of the sun on the water creating a mirage-like vision – or perhaps Dorothy and David actually are, by some mystical phenomenon, dissolving into a shimmering hologram as they step aboard their real-life Moon Singer.

* * *

"It seems I have made an impact with this new incarnation. At least with this one boy."

Other: "You have made an impact, yes. But your work – and his - has just begun. There is much more to do, more souls to encounter, more issues to resolve before your purpose, and his, is fulfilled."

"I have just scratched the surface, it seems."

Other: "The mystery is infinitely deep and the desire for answers will open a Pandora's Box of trouble as well as a treasure chest of good fortune."

"Journey on, then?"

Other: "Yes. journey on…and on…"

End of Adventure One
to be continued in Adventure Two: THE WAR CHAMBER

CPSIA information can be obtained
at www.ICGtesting.com
Printed in the USA
LVHW080322101120
671253LV00012B/591